*not her real name*

# EMILY PERKINS

## *not her real name*

## and other stories

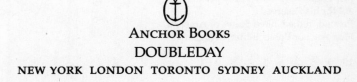

ANCHOR BOOKS
DOUBLEDAY
NEW YORK LONDON TORONTO SYDNEY AUCKLAND

AN ANCHOR BOOK
PUBLISHED BY DOUBLEDAY
a division of Bantam Doubleday Dell Publishing Group, Inc.
1540 Broadway, New York, New York 10036

ANCHOR BOOKS, DOUBLEDAY, and the portrayal of an anchor are
trademarks of Doubleday, a division of Bantam Doubleday Dell
Publishing Group, Inc.

*Not Her Real Name* was originally published in the United Kingdom
in 1996 by Picador, an imprint of Macmillan General Books. The
Anchor Books edition is published by arrangement with Picador.

Library of Congress Cataloging-in-Publication Data

Perkins, Emily, 1970–
    Not her real name and other stories / Emily Perkins. — 1st
Anchor Books ed.
        p.   cm.
        1. Young adults—Social life and customs—Fiction.   2. City and
    town life—Fiction.   I. Title.
    PR9639.3.P47N6   1997
    823—dc21                                                              97-3574
                                                                          CIP

ISBN 0-385-48664-2
Copyright © 1996 by Emily Perkins
All Rights Reserved
Printed in the United States of America
First Anchor Books Edition: August 1997

10  9  8  7  6  5  4  3  2  1

*for my family*

# contents

# *acknowledgements*

I am grateful to the friends who have encouraged and supported me during the writing of this collection; also to Bill Manhire at the Victoria University of Wellington; to Fergus Barrowman at the Victoria University Press; and to Rachel Heath and Peter Straus at Picador.

# *not her real name*

### Mud in Your Pretty Eye

Nine years later, you're leaving a bar with a friend and you see him across the wet road, getting on to a bus. From then, from the restaurant.

Francis

You always thought, Francis, rhymes with answers. Which it doesn't, really. But you'd change the s of answers to be soft like his name. Francis, Francis, there's no answers. It was a walking rhyme. A home from the bus-stop rhyme. The rhyme of a fifteen-year-old girl who could feel sad every time she thought of that soft s.

Hands in gloves in the hot water in the sink, you'd turn around and be surprised again, every time, when you saw his face. His eyes crinkled up and were almost lost when he laughed. His laugh was nearly silent and you tried to match it. You and your friend Thea had developed the habit of snorting whenever you laughed. You tried desperately to curb this around him. At the restaurant. You never thought

of it as going to work, you thought of it as going to see
Francis. You barely remembered that you were a dishwasher.
*Brideshead Revisited* was on television at the time.

You were not your usual self around Francis. None of the
cackle, the shrieking, the tough-girl acts that you and Thea
lurched around school and town with. You shrank, you
backed off, you revealed nothing. If you smiled it was
anxiously, if you spoke it was so softly that people said,
What? Eh? Speak louder. You were in love with this feeling
of self-consciousness. You wanted so much that the constant
holding of breath could bring tears to your eyes. The only
freedom you allowed yourself was imaginary. Elaborate
fantasies you dared yourself to get lost in while Francis
banged in and out of the kitchen, carrying plates, scraping
them, arguing with the chef. You thought maybe your day-
dreams would be strong enough that he could read your
mind, would look at you, know, love you. Or maybe your
body would reach out, involuntarily, necessarily, and save
itself on his thin arms. This never happened, of course. You
were fifteen. Nothing ever did.

Very thin, with wispy kind of no-colour hair, not tall,
pale, dark-circled eyes, cheekbones. Cheekbones. Every
angle you yourself did not possess was there in his cheekbones. You can't even remember the colour of his eyes.
Probably blue, some cold colour. He dressed like he knew
nothing about fashion and cared even less. You loved this
gap in his knowledge, this laziness, this flaw. You thought
nobody else could see how beautiful he was.

What happened was entirely predictable, though you never predicted it. After you'd been at the restaurant for four months, Francis left. He had exams at university and he quit his waitering job. You didn't even know it was going to happen until he said, Last fucking time I have to serve up this shit. What? you asked but nobody heard you. Why? and you felt your eyes get hot and you felt dizzy and you felt like running out, now, or saying, You're wrong, making a mistake, it's me I'm here, you can't, no. But the same thing happened, nothing. Nothing at all. And he left, he smiled your way and left, and you stayed on through the summer until March when your family moved to Auckland.

## Art Class

Hey Cody

How are you? I miss you. How's Auckland? Things here are OK. I want to leave school but not allowed. Mum's spazzing out because I told her I quit smoking – stupid – then she found a packet in my room. I miss you. Julie's OK but she never wants to wag school to watch *Prisoner*. There was a drug raid last week and Robert Stone got caught with an ounce in his locker. His dad is really pissed off because he's a cop and he caught Robert once before. Sucked. I can't wait for the August holidays. When are you coming to stay? Are there any OK guys at your school? GROSS the art teacher Mr O'Donnell just came over to see what I was

doing, we call him Stiff O'Donnell because he gawks at the
girls all the time he is so disgusting, plus he says Far Out all
the time like he thinks he's really cool or something. What
A Dick. Anyway, the mid-year dance is on next week, I'm
gonna go. I asked Celia Fox if she wants to go with me. I
really like her. Is that weird? I mean, I don't think it is, well,
I do a bit, but – does it weird you out? I don't really want to
be a Lesbian or anything, God I hate that word, but I never
felt anything the whole time I went out with Paul, I mean
he was a useless kisser but I think even if he wasn't I still
would have felt nothing. I guess I like girls more than boys.
Well, that's OK, I'm not gonna get too freaked out, write
back soon and tell me what you think. I've got this great
dress to wear, it's purple kind of plasticky stuff, quite short,
Mum'll spew. Yuck Stiff O'Donnell is perving I better go.
Tell me what you think.

love Thea

PS she said yes

It took Cody two weeks to answer Thea's letter. She started
about four before she made it sound all right. What really
worried her, though, was something she couldn't say in a
letter. In the August holidays she went down to stay with
Thea, who was going out with Celia Fox by now, and
looking forward to term three starting so they could be the
scandal of the school. Cody and Thea got Celia, a seventh
former, to buy them some wine one night and they went
and drank it in the park. Celia went home for dinner and

Cody and Thea sat on the swings, talking. Thea told Cody that just because she liked girls, it didn't mean she was attracted to her. Cody was hugely relieved. Then Thea said not to assume that she wasn't, either, and started laughing so hard she nearly fell off her swing, which did big loopy curves out over the grass. Cody laughed too and swung her swing higher and they spent the rest of the evening there winding each other up and enjoying it more than they ever had before.

This is years ago now. Cody remembers it when Thea rings her up to tell her she's met a new woman. Her name is Thea too. Cody thinks this is very bizarre and one of the hazards of having same-sex relationships. She doesn't want to say this though in case Thea thinks she's been uptight about the whole thing all along.

—Imagine a couple both called Thea, says Thea. —Isn't it awful? One of the hazards of same-sex relationships, I suppose.

—Do you and Thea want to come for dinner this week? asks Cody.

### Thea & Cody on August Holidays

> It was the boat sheds
> in winter
> & we ran out of
> that terrible play

the invitation read
danger
no climbing
on roof

we'd have slept there
we said, passing
a joint
between us

before the rain started
dreaming California

## What Happens Next

The Saturday after Cody sees Francis at the bus-stop, she goes to a party with Thea and Thea. It's a long time since Cody's been to a party. This one is in a warehouse off Cuba Street. There is a DJ playing reggae music and a lot of white people dancing to it. Cody is glad she brought her whisky.

—Something something KITCHEN something, shouts Thea at Cody.

—WHAT, shouts Cody, —WHERE?

She follows Thea into a small, brightly lit converted office. There is a bench, a sink and a stove-top element thing over which knives are heating. Thea helps herself to a bottle of wine left by somebody. Three people leave, shutting the door. It is much quieter.

—Thank fuck, says Thea, —I've got to talk to you. I think Thea's having an affair with a cycle courier.

—Oh no, says Cody. She lights a cigarette. —Male or female?

—Female, says Thea. —Which is worse, I think.

—Are you sure it's happening? asks Cody.

—No, well I am, I haven't asked her, but you know she'll only lie anyway. I'm pretty sure, oh shit, Code, I'll really miss her if we break up.

—Now hang on, hang on, says Cody. She passes Thea a paper napkin to wipe her face. She goes round the corner of the table to hug Thea and as she does the door opens and Francis walks into the room.

—Sorry, says Francis. —Bad timing. Hi.

It's a question really, he's not sure that he knows her, or if he does, from where. A lot of people are looking familiar to him these days. But he's interrupted something so he's just going to grab a plastic cup and leave.

—Wasn't that— starts Thea, wiping her nose on the lining of her suede jacket.

—Mm? says Cody. —Who? Do you want to go now?

—No, says Thea. —I don't want to leave Thea here. That cycle bitch might show. Can I have some lipstick?

They spend a minute putting Thea back together again and then walk out to the party. Thea finds Thea and they dance while Cody walks over to the window not looking for Francis.

He finds her anyway, and this is what he says.

—Leo Tolstoy and his brother believed anything they wished would come true if they could stand in a corner and not think of a white bear.

Cody feels her rib cage expand, contract, expand, contract. She lights another cigarette off the butt of the one she's just smoked. She has a mouthful of whisky, making sure not to spill any down her chin. Her hands shake. She tightens her grip on the windowsill.

—I know you from somewhere, he says.

—Um, says Cody, —I think we might have worked in the same restaurant once, ages ago now, about ten years ago or something, is your name Francis?

—Yeah. He smiles. —What's yours again?

—Cody, says Cody.

—What? says Francis.

—Cody, she says again, hating this. —C–O–D–Y.

—Cody? he says.

—Yeah. She's feeling sick now even without the whisky, wondering where her personality's gone. She could have sworn she had it on her when she left the house.

—Visions of Cody, he smiles.

—Yeah, says Cody. —I never read it yet.

For a while they stand there at the window next to each other not saying anything. Cody looks around the room at the other women there. They all look completely gorgeous. She glances carefully over at Francis. He's looking straight ahead, sucking the rim of his plastic cup with red wine in it. Cody realizes with relief that she is bored, and walks away.

—

But here she is now at the end of the party and there's only a handful of people left. Thea and Thea have gone home. The cycle courier never showed up. Cody is talking to a red-haired woman about Virginia Woolf and trying to sound informed but not pretentious while keeping Francis in her peripheral vision. She got Thea to make some enquiries for her earlier on and found out he's not with anyone, he just got back from overseas. Which potentially places him in a high-risk category but at least he's available. Cody can't get over how he looks exactly the same. She's not sure whether this is good or bad.

—Ugh, said Thea, —He looks like he crawled out from under a rock. I thought you'd gotten over that Brideshead cheekbone thing.

—I did, said Cody. —I did get over it.

Cody sees him going for his coat and manages to look as if she got up to leave first. There is an art to this manoeuvre and she has to concentrate hard, which is not easy after three and a half hours of whisky and forty-five minutes of leftover beer.

She hears him behind her on the stairs. Once she's outside she stops and looks up at the stars. The night is clear and very cold. She is wide awake. She looks at him, surprised. She smiles.

—Hi, he says.

—Hi.

They walk together down the street, hands in pockets, ears ringing from the music. Everything else is still. They reach the taxi stand.

In the taxi he asks her if she wants to go back to his place. She can't believe it's been this easy. She says OK, still looking surprised, smiling a small smile.

Actually it's not his place, it's his brother's who is away for the weekend. This is a further stroke of luck. Cody does not like to encounter strange flatmates in the morning. The mornings are awkward enough as it is. Francis pours them each a glass of wine and puts a record on. He touches Cody's face. He says, —I remember you.

They go to bed.

—Well, says Thea the next day, —how was it?

—Good, says Cody. —I think. I can't remember much.

—So, says Thea, —what happens next?


### Swimming Back Upstream

> but here's a
> new mark
>
> on my
> white flesh
>
> fingers
> or mouth
>
> have
> bruised it fresh
>
> and I want
> to laugh

and I want
to run

and I want to
show you

what you
have done


## *In Case* Interview *Ever Wants to Know*

Because there are at least eight other things she should be
doing, Cody spends the afternoon compiling the guest list
for her Ideal Dinner Party. She has a strong sense that,
although she's only a waitress right now, some day magazines will want to know this kind of information from her.
Her Desert Island Discs; Night-Table Reading; Who Is The
Sexiest Man In Politics, etc.

She decides to limit herself to six guests, three of each
sex. She starts with Susan Sarandon. Susan is one of Cody's
favourite actresses and it's apparent that not only is she
talented and beautiful, she's also a smart political thinker.
Plus she's played a lot of waitresses. Cody feels Susan will
be an excellent contributor to dinner party conversation.

Susan Sarandon
Al Gore

Al Gore? He *is* the Sexiest Man In Politics, but maybe a little
earnest. Cody's unsure how his environmental stance will

suit the style of evening she wants – sharp, funny, an element of risk. Leave him in for the time being. But no Tipper.

That couple the film *Lorenzo's Oil* was about. Real people who changed the world through love and determination. Whoa, then Susan will be at dinner with the woman she played in a movie. Does it matter? Are there too many Americans so far?

Mother Teresa? – maybe not.

It disturbs Cody how hard she's having to think about this. You'd imagine it would be easy enough to rattle off six heroes from the top of your head. But it involves more than that. It involves balance, precision, a successful dynamic. Cody's disappointed she can't think of more famous people in Science, or Classical Music. What about Anita Hill? She's another American, true, but she'd definitely get on well with Susan. Maybe Al could do something nasty to Clarence Thomas on her behalf. Does Al have anything to do with the Supreme Court? Surely he's got some influence.

> Susan Sarandon
> Al Gore
> *Lorenzo's Oil* couple
> ~~Mother Teresa~~
> Anita Hill

The couple from *Lorenzo's Oil* are standing on shaky ground. What Cody needs now is a man. Someone older perhaps, erudite, charming, powerful. Someone witty and wise who can offer the benefit of experience. Someone Al could learn from, and the others could be grateful to have had the opportunity to meet. In literature? Politics? Prince Rainier? Gore Vidal? Gielgud?

On the other hand, Cody does need someone to help with the dishes. And there's always the possibility of one last drink, a walk by the sea, an undeniable electric attraction that demands to be fulfilled –

> Susan Sarandon
> Al Gore
> ~~Lorenzo's Oil couple~~
> ~~Mother Teresa~~
> Anita Hill
> Daniel Day-Lewis
> Brad Pitt
> Johnny Depp

—

The weekend after Francis, Cody and Thea go to breakfast. They try and figure out which of the couples surrounding them just met the night before. Cody needs to talk about Francis.

—I can't stop thinking about him, she says.

—That's bad, says Thea.

—I know.

—You need to fuck someone else.

—Who? says Cody, looking around the room.

—Anyone, Thea says. —There are other guys. Anyone. Just don't obsess about thingy.

—Francis.

—Francis. What kind of a name is that for a guy?

—I am obsessing, aren't I? Cody slops her coffee into the saucer.

—Yes, says Thea.

—I'm enjoying it. I can't help it. I'm out of control.

—Crap, says Thea.

Their food arrives. Cody wonders if the waiter is attractive enough to sleep with. She decides that he isn't.

—And, she says, —I keep remembering things.

Thea sighs. —Spare me the details.

—No, but, like the mascara.

—What?

—Well, says Cody, —There was this mascara on his bedside table. Do you think he's a cross-dresser?

—Were there any feather boas lying around?

—No. Um, I don't think so.

—Cody, you moron. He's not a cross-dresser, he's got a fucking girlfriend.

—But you said he was single, Cody says, feeling a tantrum coming on.

—Well, I don't know for sure. But make-up is a sure sign of a girlfriend.

—Oh.

—Either that or he's a New Romantic.

—I'd rather he had a girlfriend.

—What are you going to do tonight?

—Get drunk.

—And?

—And fuck someone else.

—Good girl.

### Regarding Francis

I sit in my room
thinking & smoking
thinking & smoking &
whisky all day

I want to write a story
about a man I met
met & went to bed with
went to bed with & left

But it's raining & cold
& the sky is all grey
the words are too hard
the memories not old

there's something there's something
it's too hard to say


### How Do I Love Thee

It's coming up to Thea and Thea's four year anniversary.
Cody goes shopping on Saturday morning for a present. She
looks at matching bath robes, matching latte bowls, matching photograph frames. All these are too expensive. She
settles for bath oil. As she watches the shop assistant
wrapping it, she feels a fist of envy clench in her stomach.

She snatches the parcel from across the counter and shoves it deep into her bag. She forgets about it until Thea comes around that night. There's been a fight.

It goes like this.

Thea and Thea are having breakfast. Thea wants to go for a walk to Cody's place. She rings and gets the answerphone but decides to go anyway. She needs to get out of the house.

—I'm going for a walk, she tells Thea.

Thea looks up from her toast. —Do you love me?

—I love you, darling, says Thea, putting on her sunglasses.

—Good.

—*Were* you seeing that cycle courier? asks Thea, smiling.

—Thea. Please.

—Were you? she asks, standing in the kitchen doorway now, leaning against the doorframe, casual.

—No. Of course not. God.

—OK, says Thea, —I'm going for a walk now.

She doesn't move from the doorway.

Thea gets up and starts clearing the table. —I love you, Thee, she says.

—Thee, thou, thine, says Thea from the doorway.

Thea giggles. —With all my worldly goods I Thee endow.

—Were you? asks Thea again.

—What? says Thea, scrubbing bacon grease off the grill.

—You did, didn't you, says Thea, clinging to the doorframe now, her fingernails picking at the paint. —You did fuck her. I'm not stupid.

—Thea, says Thea, warning.

—She's a bimbo, you know that?

—Leave it alone, says Thea, pushing past Thea to the living-room.

—I'm going for a walk now, Thea calls after her.

She and Cody go to a movie that night. Thea cries loudly through most of it. When the lights go on at the end her face is red and puffy.

—Can I stay at your place tonight? she asks Cody.

—No, says Cody, —go and make up with Thea. Here, she remembers, fishing in her bag, —give her this. I bought it for both of you.

—Are you sure? says Thea. —She might not want to talk to me.

—One way to find out, says Cody.

She leaves Thea at a taxi stand and walks home alone as the rain starts to spit under the streetlights.

### Cody Makes Sure

There's nothing more boring than people telling you their dreams. God, no. Anyone'll tell you that. And everyone thinks their dreams must be the most interesting, the most symbolic, the best evidence of their inner complexity. Jesus, the number of people who would never tell you about their sex lives but go on about their dreams all day long. It's daytime, for Christ's sake! Wake up! Nobody cares! Besides, there's only about seven dreams really, that just slip from head to head in the night. Tramps.

I'm having a baby
My teeth are crumbling
Wow, I can fly
I'm having sex with
    a) person you find repulsive
    b) person you're related to
    c) person you thought you'd gotten over by now
I'm having sex with
    a) man of your dreams
    b) woman of your dreams
    c) animal of your dreams (surely not)
I'm driving a car and it's out of control
I'm on stage naked, late, and I don't know my lines.

So, dreams are something I've vowed never to talk about. I'm not going to bore you stupid with my extended nightly soap operas. There's just one thing I want to be clear about, though: I have never, *ever* dreamed about Francis. Ever.

## The Ditch

It's been a rocky week. On Tuesday, Thea announced to Cody that she and Thea are splitting up. She's worried that they're becoming co-dependent – whatever *that* means.

—It's that four year thing, said Thea.

—Um, said Cody, who can't remember having a relationship that's lasted more than four weeks.

And then Thea said she was going to Sydney in a month.

—To live?
—Yup.
—You're fucking joking.
—Nup.

Thea will stay with her cousin until she can get a job and a place of her own. She's serious about leaving. Cody does not welcome this piece of news.

—How fantastic. I'm so jealous, you'll have such a great time.
—Yeah, I'm a bit nervous.
—Oh, you'll be fine. I better start saving so I can visit.

Cody spends that evening going over her bank statements and crying. She has fifty-four dollars and the rent's due this week. She doesn't understand why she's a waitress. She doesn't understand anything anymore. She goes to the bottle store and buys a twenty-eight-dollar bottle of vodka.

Wednesday, Thursday and Friday Cody says she's busy whenever Thea calls. On Saturday morning Thea turns up with a bunch of grapes.

—I'm not sick, says Cody.
—Why are you avoiding me? asks Thea.
—I'm not.
—Cody.
—What? What? There's nothing going on.
—You're mad at me.
—I'm not.

The kettle whistles and overflows.

—Fucking screaming noise, says Cody.

Thea turns the kettle off and makes tea.

—OK, says Cody, —I hate you. You're leaving.

—I'll miss you, says Thea —Just don't ruin this last bit.

—Christ, Thea. Why is it so hard for me to let people go?

—I don't know, darling. But you'd better get over it.

That night Cody dreams she is a little girl again.

### Tender Callus

talked all night
drank till four
taxi to somewhere
clothes hit the floor

sighing & laughing
ten years isn't much
again & again &
touch touch touch

so tender he says
like sirloin she smiles
sun too bright to sleep
is callousness guile

yes Francis Francis
there's no words to say

just take me to somewhere
I'd better not stay

—

Cody shows Gene, the cook where she works, the ad she's put in the paper.

Flatmate wanted
7b Hunter St
Sat–Sun
$50pw No pets

—You're mad, says Gene. —You're going to have to stay home all weekend and you could get any kind of freak coming round. You should've just put your phone number.

—Been cut off, says Cody. —Where's the pepper grinder?

—Are you looking for a male or female? asks Gene.

—Don't care really, says Cody. —I just need the money. It'll probably be a disaster whatever sex they are.

—That's the spirit, says Gene. —Take that soup now and the fish'll be ready when you come back.

Cody knows she shouldn't be so negative about sharing her flat. She's taken her desk and an armchair out of the sunroom. There's just enough room for a double bed and a small chest of drawers. She vacuumed for the first time in about a month and scrubbed the bath. The *Woman's Weeklys* are hidden under her bed and a couple of Kundera books are lying casually on the kitchen table. She wonders what she's trying to prove. She feels her misplaced pride dragging her around the house, trying to create the image of a fabulous self-sufficient working woman. She buys fresh flowers. This is exhausting.

—See you Monday, she says to Gene at the end of the night.
—Good luck, says Gene. —Hope you don't get any psychos.

### The Gentleman Caller

All Saturday Cody waits at home for prospective flatmates to call around. It rains, and she plays patience and looks at the dead telephone. No one comes.

On Sunday she wakes up in the afternoon with a hangover. She thinks, fuck this. She leaves a note on the door and goes to the market. Coming back up her path as dark is falling, she sees someone standing in her doorway trying to read the note. She calls out, —Hi. She runs up the steps to the door. It's Francis.

She feels her tongue dry in her mouth. She can't swallow. She doesn't trust herself to speak. He looks terrified. He speaks.

—I'm sorry I didn't call you.
—I didn't give you my phone number.
—Um.
—Uh—

Cody can't find her key. She considers running back down the path, leaving Francis on the doorstep in the dark.

—Should I come in?

—Uh. Sure, I'll just – here it is – uh—

She follows him inside, turning on the lights. They stand stuck in the narrow hallway. Cody doesn't want to squeeze past Francis and he's not going anywhere on his own.

—Have you had many people through? he asks, and she realizes he is here for the flat, there's no mistake, he hasn't tracked her down, sought her out, found her. He's looking for somewhere to live.

—No, she says. —None, I mean, so far. You're the first.

—Oh. Really?

—Yeah, well, it's been raining, so—

—Right. Um, it seems really nice. Is this, um, the room here?

He gestures to the sunroom door on his right.

—Yeah, that's it, Cody says, not opening the door. —I've been here on my own, you know, I much prefer it. But, um, I need the money, I'm trying to save.

—Oh yeah? How much is the room again?

—Fifty a week.

—That's really good for so central. I mean, I haven't got a lot of money, fifty's really good.

—Do you work? asks Cody.

—Yeah, at a second-hand bookshop in town.

—Oh.

—You're a waitress, right?

—Yeah. Uh, so this is the bathroom—

Cody shows Francis around her flat, surreptitiously checking herself in every reflective surface. How can this be happening? A second-hand bookshop? Jesus Christ almighty. Jesus Christ alfuckingmighty.

—Oh and that's my room, she says, flicking her hand in the direction of her closed bedroom door. —And this is the kitchen.

—Gas oven, great. Oh, Kundera. You like him?

—Mm.

—Can I see the room that's going?

—Oh sure, sorry, here—

They stand in the empty sunroom, looking out at the night. Cody is struggling to find an etiquette for this situation. Why is he still here? Why hasn't she just said, Look, I'm sorry, what a silly mistake, I don't need a flatmate anymore, I'm moving in with my boyfriend, we're in love you know, he's asked me to marry him . . . Shit. Shit fuck.

—Well look, says Francis, —I really like this place. So, um—

—Right.

—Do you need someone in a hurry?

—Yeah, I do really, the phone's been cut off, and—

—Oh.

Well, that was clever, Cody tells herself. Bang goes your escape route. And now you look like an idiot who can't manage money. You *are* an idiot who can't manage money.

Gross financial mismanagement, that's what got you into this mess.

—Um, well I need somewhere straight away, Francis is saying, —My brother's fed up with me sleeping on his couch.

—So that wasn't your—Cody immediately regrets the reference to that night.

—Um, no, it was my brother's um room.

—Oh right.

The image Cody has been carrying around with her of Francis's girlfriend putting on mascara while Francis watches from the bed vanishes.

—Look, she says, —Do you think—

—I guess it does look like a fairly foolish idea.

—Foolish. Mm.

—Well, says Francis, —you're desperate for a flatmate—

I'm not desperate for anything thanks very much, thinks Cody.

—And, he continues, —I really need somewhere cheap and central—

That's me, thinks Cody, cheap and central.

—Also, he says, —I am the only person who's come to look.

—Well, says Cody, —I'm working nights at the moment.

—And I work days, so we wouldn't even need to see each other.

—Yeah . . . says Cody.

—Oh, says Francis, —do you smoke?

—I've just given up, says Cody. —I can't really afford it.

—Well, I'm asthmatic.

—Oh right, says Cody, trying not to smirk.

—Well, I'm willing to forget what happened between us, says Francis. —I think we could be mature about this, don't you?

—Oh, of course, says Cody. —Absolutely. No, it wouldn't be an issue.

—So what do you think?

Cody hates being asked this question.

—Um, she says, —sure. I mean, if you like the room – sure.

—I could move my stuff in tomorrow while you're at work.

—OK, fine.

—Could you leave a key in the letterbox?

—OK, sure.

—Great, says Francis, heading for the door. —Great, I'll see you tomorrow then, probably.

—OK, says Cody, —uh, see you.

She closes the door behind him, feeling dazed and a bit giddy. She waits to make sure he's got down the road and gets her coat and some money and goes to a phone box to call Thea.

—Cody, says Thea, —are you sure you know what you're doing? You sound dangerously excited. Are you smiling?

—No, says Cody, —I'm not, I'm quite rational about this, it'll be fine.

—You *are* smiling, says Thea. —I can hear it. And you're smoking. I thought you gave up.

—Just one, says Cody. —I bludged it off the guy at the bottle store. Do you think I'm crazy?

—Yes, says Thea, —I think you're an idiot.

—I am, aren't I? says Cody. —But I don't care.

—Just don't have sex with him again, says Thea.

—Of course not, says Cody. —Of course not. I'm not that stupid.

—Oh Jesus, says Thea, —would you just stop smiling?

—

Cutting Francis's hair. We sat on the steps out the front of the house. It was the first sunny weekend in a couple of weeks. I had a comb, a bowl of water, and the kitchen snips. Francis had a towel around his neck. There was music playing and the front door was open and I thought, This is it. This is it. Francis's skull was warm under my hands. He was telling some funny story about the bookshop and I was laughing and I snorted and I didn't care. He leant back against my knees and I must have lost concentration because I cut his ear. He kind of yelped and there was a lot of blood, more than seemed natural, and I couldn't stop laughing. This was the wrong thing to do. He jumped up and knocked over the bowl of water and it ran down the steps looking dark and red in the sun. He ran into the house to get a sticking plaster and tripped over because the dark inside was such a contrast to the winter brightness and he couldn't see. I stayed on the steps, squinting, feeling guilty for not feeling guilty. Francis came blinking back outside and I apologized. He wouldn't let me near him again with the scissors. I didn't point out that I'd only finished cutting one side.

*Flood*

In the third week after Francis moved in, there is a terrible rainstorm. It starts on Wednesday night and keeps coming all day Thursday. When Francis gets home from work on Thursday evening he discovers that the sunroom roof is leaking and his bedroom's flooded.

—Bloody hell, he says, standing in the middle of his damp rug. —Bloody hell. His voice gets louder. —Bloody bloody *bloody*.

—You sound like my father, Cody says, coming into Francis's room.

—It's bloody soaked, says Francis, his voice under control again. —It's leaking all over the bloody place. Look.

—Oh shit, says Cody. —Whoops.

—What do you mean? says Francis. —Did you know about this?

—No, says Cody, —Of course not. I just mean, you know, bummer.

—Bummer, says Francis. —Bummer? Look at this. Bummer? It's fucked. It's soaked. My bed— He goes to his bed and wrings out a corner of the sheet, —my bed is fucking soaking. Where am I going to sleep?

As soon as the question is out there they both avoid

looking at each other. Cody backs out of Francis's room and down the hall.

—Well, she calls from the kitchen, opening and closing cupboard doors, not looking for anything, just needing the covering noise, —You could always stay in my room. I won't be home till late.

—Uh, calls Francis from his room, pulling his bed out from the wet wall, —yeah. Well I might have to.

—That's fine, calls Cody. —I'm going to work now – um, see you later.

—Bye, Francis mutters. —Bloody, *bloody* hell.

Francis drags his mattress on to its side and turns the heater towards it. He checks it every fifteen minutes. It's getting drier, but not dry enough.

Cody stays after work for a special coffee with Gene.

—Go easy on the brandy, says Gene. —Cigarette?

—Love one, says Cody. —Thanks.

When Cody gets home the lights are all out. She opens her bedroom door quietly. Francis is in the bed, on his side, asleep. She gets her T-shirt and goes to change in the bathroom.

Francis opens his eyes. He hears Cody brushing her teeth. He moves further towards the edge of the bed. Cody gets into bed very carefully. She lies on her back as far to the other side of the bed as she can go, her hands crossed over her chest. She tries to regulate her breathing.

Neither of them moves a muscle all night. Neither of them gets much sleep. Francis gets out of bed at 7 am. Cody stretches out at last. She swaps her pillow for his. The rain stops.

### Look, Francis

she wants it &
she wants it now
she wants it
& she'll tell you how

she wants it in
the afternoon
she wants it slow
& quick & soon

she wants it soft
she wants it rough
she wants it
till she's had enough

she wants it loud
& silenced too
but more than it
she must have you

—

Three weekends after the flood, Francis and Cody spend the evening at home together. It is very windy outside and every now and then the house shudders. There is a bottle of wine nearly empty on the floor between them. Francis is berating Cody for having enjoyed a recently fashionable book which is not only sentimental, falsely optimistic and clumsily written—

—But face it, it's also fundamentally morally flawed.

—*You're* morally flawed.

—Don't be so facile.

—Don't be so anal.

—Jargon-monger.

—Pedant.

—Fashion victim.

—Bore.

They glare at each other across the room. Francis clears his throat.

—Look, he says, —We could sit here hurling insults at each other all night but I'd much rather go to bed with you.

—I'd much rather eat my own vomit.

—I find *that* hard to believe.

—I find *you* hard to believe.

—Stop it.

Cody pours herself some more wine, finishing the bottle. She is desperate for a cigarette. She sighs. The sigh goes on longer than she expected and she is suddenly afraid she might cry. She stands up. Francis stands up. He looks out the window.

—I'm sorry.

—For what, says Cody.

—That was a particularly charmless proposal. I didn't mean to assume—.

Cody goes to the window and stands behind Francis. She strokes the back of his head, down to his neck. She sees Francis's reflection in the window. He has closed his eyes.

—Don't assume anything, she tells him. —And don't talk.

She leads him carefully to his bedroom. He opens his eyes.

—

An aerial photograph of a city at night-time.

Dear Cody

How are you darling? I miss you. I miss Thea too, more than I expected. I might have a job! – details later if it works out. When are you coming over? I *miss* you.

Thea.

PS I love Sydney.
PPS Are you being careful?

*Bonfire*

In the dream there is a field. Francis is in the field. She gets closer and she can see the food, the fruit and leaves and meats spilling out of the horn. The Horn of Plenty from her childhood books. A large cream shell lying on the dark grass. *Viands*, she thinks, *nectar*. Francis is back, crouching by the horn, eating everything that comes out. He's wearing his yellow raincoat. He's eating and eating and he's not getting any bigger.

> I got plenty of nothing
> Nothing's plenty for me

Cody sings these lines all day after she remembers the dream.

She doesn't imagine Francis to be the kind of guy who feels sexual frustration. He doesn't seem to be driven by anything like that. She wishes that he was.

I'm the guy here, she decides. It makes sense the more she thinks about it. The two times they've had sex, she's fallen straight to sleep after while Francis has lain awake. She can tell by the darker than usual circles under his eyes in the mornings. Also, she can drink more than him. Which is not to say she can hold it better, but she can keep going long after he's had enough. She knows this is not her most attractive feature.

She's not the guy. She knows that too. She doesn't even know what a guy is, other than Guy Fawkes. She wishes she was more politically active.

She goes to bed at night determined not to dream about Francis. She doesn't. She doesn't. She does.


### And Had Nothing to do With The Sea

Francis comes home from the bookshop. From the path he can hear that Cody is playing her Kurt Weill record. Again.

Christ, he thinks, if I have to listen to 'Surabaya Johnny' one more time I'll smash something.

—Hi, Cody calls from her room. She's getting ready to go to work.

Francis goes into his room and shuts the door. He feels like slamming it but restrains himself. Control, he thinks, calm.

> —I was young, God I'd just turned sixteen—

He can hear Cody singing along, loudly and not very well. He gets the shoe polish from under his bed and starts working on his shoes. He is rubbing furiously when Cody sticks her lipsticked face around the door. He starts, flushes, tries for some reason to cover the shoes with the rag. He feels as if he's been caught masturbating.

—I'm off, Cody says. —Have a good night.

—Yeah, he says. —See you.

He sees her out his window walking down the path, still singing. She's waving her arms in time.

> —You said a lot, Johnny
> All one big lie, Johnny
> You cheated me blind, Johnny
> From the minute we . . .

Her voice trails after her as she disappears around the corner. He should never have slept with her. He should never have moved in. What a stupid mistake. He doesn't even know her. He hates this messy complication of his life. Bloody mess. At least she's clean.

He goes to her room and stands outside the door. It would be easy to open it, walk in, look in drawers, the wardrobe, the desk. Under the bed. Get to know her that way. Cheat. This is ridiculous, he thinks, looking at himself in the hall mirror on the way back to his room. He looks tired. Older? Probably.

He falls onto his bed. The tin of shoe polish gets him directly between the shoulder blades. Twisting around, he knocks it upside down. There is a thick black streak on his blanket. He throws the shoe polish on the floor. It wheels around leaving fainter black traces before it settles. Francis gets under the blankets with his clothes still on. He counts to a hundred. His breathing slows.

When he wakes up it is dark and the room is cold. He feels a moment of lurching panic. He thinks about going into town. He could have a coffee at Cody's café. Sit, talk, walk home together.

He has a bath.

He reads a book.

—

A painting of a bowl of fruit.

Dearest Code
    Thea says she saw you in a jeweller's shop with some weedy looking guy. *Tell me she's joking.* I'm working for one of Sydney's top production companies – as a script editor. Scares me shitless. I love it. I miss you, write.
                           love Thea.

*The Crowded Empty Bar*

inside Cody
small & still
sits & waits
an act of will

outwardly, she
runs the race
spins around
for each new face

mantra chants
the inside child
hums her hymn
is meek & mild

the hurricane
outside the eye
shows no sign
does not know why

Francis is a thumb
I want to suck

—

Cody gets home from work to find Francis and a friend
drinking coffee in the living-room. The friend's name is
Marc. Marc with a c. Cody's seen it written down by the

telephone. Not for the first time, she wonders if Francis might be gay.

—How was work? asks Francis.

—Fine, says Cody. She doesn't really hear him. She can't take her eyes off the back of Marc's head. Marc. Marc. There's something disturbing about the name. Like Jon without an h. Or Shayne with a y. Marc. Spelt backwards, it makes cram. A real word. This makes it seem like code. Code for what? Cram, cram. Trying to break the Code. OK, so her own name is enough of a liability. She shouldn't laugh at other people's. But *Marc* – it's like biting tinfoil.

—Um, I'm going to have a bath, says Cody.

—Fine, says Francis.

From the bath she can hear them talking. About what? She has no idea what guys talk about when they're alone. Sport? Sex? Not those two. Dungeons and dragons maybe. Or the relative merits of MMP and STV. Her? Doubt it.

—Night, she calls on her way to bed.

—Night, Francis and Marc call after her.

It is three o'clock before she hears the front door close.

—

—I'm pregnant, says Gene at work on Monday night.

—Oh boy, says Cody. —Is that a good thing or a bad thing?

—Both, I guess, says Gene, slapping a steak down on the grill.

Cody looks at her closely to see if she's changed. She's read that during pregnancy your hair is at its glossy best and

your skin is glowing. But Gene's ponytail is as limp as ever
and she always glows at work anyway, from the heat in the
kitchen.

—Are you throwing up yet? asks Cody.

—Nah, says Gene. —Soon maybe. Hey—she looks at
Cody, worried, —does it show?

She stands side-on to Cody. She's wearing her T-shirt
that says *do* i *look as if* i *care* on the front, and leggings.

—No, says Cody. —Don't worry about it.

—Good, says Gene. —That means I don't have to tell
him yet. He'll do a runner as soon as he finds out.

—So what are you going to do? asks Cody.

—Go ahead with it and pretend he might change, says
Gene. —I want to have the baby. Even if I'm on my own.

—You're brave, says Cody.

—And stupid, says Gene.

—Yeah, says Cody, —and stupid.


Cody spends the next day at the library reading international
magazines. She mostly skims through the articles, but reads
the short stories in *Buzz* magazine and *The New Yorker*. She
is relieved to discover that many of these deal with the same
sort of man trouble problems as she has got. There's a whole
bunch of American women out there writing about stuff
she can relate to. The No-Good-Men Genre. Cody feels
reassured, part of a global sorority of single women. Things
can't be so bad if they have the same situations in San
Francisco and Chicago as they do in Wellington. At least
they're all in it together.

No. Wait a minute. Cody stops cold. It is not in fact a good thing if man trouble is an international phenomenon. It is in fact a disaster. The one thing she's been relying on is the fantasy of a different breed of man overseas. Every Antipodean girl's dream – Mr Europe! – Mr Africa! – Mr Mediterranean! – take your places, please. Now Cody knows that this will never be a reality. Even if she could ever save enough money to go to New York, she'd still be scouring the streets for a halfway decent man. Shit. Looks like she's going to have to ditch romance and hold out for the fast-track, power-dressing career.

She leaves the magazines on the floor and scuffs her feet all the way down the street to the café.


### Which Face

thirteen at a table
Francis the last
no one to kiss
left with the glass

port passed round
not immune
towards the star
right through moon

here Francis
have this mask

heart sees face
this your task

have an answer
have some air
from this distance
you're so fair

—

Francis has woken up too early. He pulls a jersey on over his pyjamas and shivers. The sky is milky blue. He traces a line curving up and around in the condensation on the window. He worries that the shape he's drawn is too phallic. He worries that he worries too much.

In the kitchen he tries to make coffee without disturbing Cody. She'd probably sleep through a siren anyway, he thinks, as the percolator hisses over onto the gas flame. He searches the bench for a teaspoon. Old teabags, dirty knives, crumbs. Standards are slipping. On the table he finds a teaspoon under a piece of paper with writing on it.

> Mark called twice
> sorry forgot to tell you
> We need soap!
> C.

He wonders how long the note's been there. He thinks about what he has to do at work today. He's trying to make some changes to the bookshop. Get rid of some of the trash and concentrate on the upmarket, cerebral and quirky. He has a sudden vision of himself as a turn-of-the-century shop clerk, tight collar and pinched brow, pushing pieces of paper around on a desk. He wishes he were back overseas. Maybe he'll get drunk tonight.

He stops outside Cody's door. Without thinking, he opens it and slowly steps into her room. She's almost hidden beneath her blankets, face buried in a pillow. He can't see her breathing. He imagines going to shake her, giving her a fright, seeing her uncomposed morning face open in alarm. He doesn't do it. He doesn't do that sort of thing. But he thinks it, which makes him feel guilty enough.

He sits gently on the end of Cody's bed and watches her sleep. She moves her feet a little bit. Nothing much happens. He leaves her room, forgetting on purpose to close the door. On his way to work, he smiles when he imagines her waking up.

—

A black and white photograph of two schoolgirls on a road.

Cody

    Anyone would think you'd disappeared off the face of the earth. I called your machine, your voice is still on the tape. Is that guy hiding you under the floorboards? or boiling you up on the stove? Ninety-nine per cent of women are murdered in their own homes. Or something like that.

    Thea

## I'm Giving You a Longing Look

Cody wakes from a late-morning dream. The room is hot.
She's still heavy and slow from sleep, but her mind is clear.
She knows there's something she has to do. Francis, she
thinks, which is nothing new. There is something different
now though. She feels a pulse somewhere which tells her
she's going to do something. She doesn't want to think what
it is. She just wants to get there.

She has a bath and gets dressed to music she and Thea
used to listen to at school.

> Here's some mud in your pretty eye
> But please drop in if you're passing by
> I'll tell you how much I hate you girl
> Perhaps it isn't true, perhaps it isn't true

She brushes her hair, humming, smiling at herself in the
mirror. Tears come into her eyes. She misses Thea. She'll
write to her, after she's done this.

Walking into town she wonders if she's been kidnapped
by the FBI and brainwashed as a sleeper. I must kill John
Lennon, I must kill John Lennon, she mutters, then laughs
out aloud. She feels hysteria welling up and breathes down
to control it. She realizes she's heading straight for Francis's
bookshop. What's she doing? This is stupid – she's about to
turn back but she gets rid of the thought, she doesn't think
anything, the song runs through her head.

*not her real name*

> To those who look snide
> And those who connive
> I say love cannot be contrived
> Love cannot be denied

She's scaring herself now, and walking still, getting closer
and closer. It's a mistake, it's wrong. No. Just get there.

> And if you ask me to explain
> The rules of the game
> I'll say you missed the point again

She walks into the bookshop and up to the desk where
Francis is sitting. There's no one else there.

—Hi, Cody, he says.

—Hi, Francis, she says. She squeezes in past the desk and
stands behind his chair. For seven seconds she doesn't touch
him. Then her hands reach over his shoulders and down his
chest. Her mouth is very close to his right ear. One hand
finds it way up inside his jersey. The other feels the worn
leather of his belt. She kisses his throat. He turns and stands
and the chair falls over and her back is against the wall and
they are kissing each other. She twists him around and she
holds him to the wall, holds his hands to the wall, kisses him
and hears someone behind her. She lets him go. He is
confused.

—Sorry, he says to the customer.

She isn't sorry. She laughs and says goodbye and leaves
the shop.

Francis reaches in his desk drawer and pulls out his
inhaler. He gulps mouthfuls of Ventolin. The customer asks

him if he's got anything by Julian Barnes and he says Never heard of him, when of course he has, he's read everything he's written, but the only one he can remember right now is *Talking It Over*, and he decides that's what they've got to do.

When Cody gets home from work that night Francis is in the living-room smoking a cigarette.

—What about your asthma? says Cody.

—I don't care, says Francis.

—OK, says Cody.

—I'm going to move out, says Francis.

—OK, says Cody.

—It's not healthy, says Francis.

—OK, says Cody.

They look at each other. Cody lights a cigarette off the end of Francis's and steps away again.

—I want you, says Francis.

—Do you, says Cody.

—Yes, says Francis.

—Really, says Cody.

—Yes, says Francis.

—I suppose you want to consume me, says Cody.

—Yes, says Francis.

—Well, says Cody, —you can try.

Later, you can't sleep. You don't care. You reach over Cody for a cigarette. You light it and cough. You lie on your back blowing smoke into the dark above you. Cody wakes up. You pass her the cigarette. You smile at her.

—Cody, you say.

She smiles back. —What? she says.

—Cody, you say. —C–O–D–Y.

—Visions of Cody, she says, handing you back the cigarette.

—Yeah, you say, still smiling, —Every day I write the book.

# *barking*

So I'm in my drama class, right? And I think like I want to be this very cool actor-type, Brando or James Dean or something – and I could have been too, you know, I really could. But the stupid dumb fuck drama class I'm taking is some idiot thing run by idiots and we spend all this time looking for our centres or relaxing or rubbing each other. It's pretty disgusting I'm telling you. But still I was sticking it out because I thought, you know, this is how people get discovered, who's going to know I've got a great face and a mean snarl if nobody ever sees it? But this day, where things really started getting rotten, I'd just about had enough. And we're in Clown class, the worst possible thing ever.

Let me tell you something about clowns – they're sick. Anyone who takes a fucking Clown class ought to be locked up. So, Mr Jones, what do you do? Oh, I'm a clown teacher. Right, good one. And these people really think they're contributing, that's the sad thing, they really think they're doing the world a service by teaching losers like me how to

Find Their Clown. Our clown teacher, she was worse than most at that stupid Drama Centre – one of those deadly serious people who pretend they've got a really 'natural' and 'spontaneous' sense of fun, and it's all about learning how to play 'just like you did when you were a natural, happy, unafraid child'. Well, I'm so sorry for not growing up with the Waltons Family. Anyway, that's her. You can imagine the type? Wheatgerm coming out her ears, forced maniac grin on her stupid face, probably goes home at night and cries in the dark. Probably has kids with eating disorders. Lucinda the witch.

So, I'm in Lucinda's class, and today we're going to improvise with our clowns. That means we're going to put our stupid clown costumes and our stupid clown make-up on, and with everybody watching we're going to make something up. Something 'child-like' and 'spontaneous' and 'delightfully funny'. In other words, we're going to make total fuckwits of ourselves.

And sure enough, we sit through about eight people doing their little clown act, and I'm just about asleep this is so deadly. There's one girl that's quite funny but that's only because she's got this really huge arse and seeing her try and do mime with her black tights on and her big old butt bouncing all over is pretty good. She's the least graceful thing you've ever seen, tiptoeing around like one of those hippo ballerinas. Anyway, Lucinda must have guessed that my snickering is hardly out of child-like joy and wonder, because she picks on me next.

—That was really special, Ginger, she says, —Thank you

for letting us see that. Dog? Perhaps you'd like some play-time now?

I am serious, that's how she talks. I better explain about the names – they're our clown names. Janice or June or whatever Hippogirl's name is, made the original choice of Ginger – she has red hair. I mean, Jesus, I thought we were supposed to be encouraging imagination here. My clown name is Dog. I know it's kind of weird but it's better than my first choice, which was Cunt. I didn't tell Lucinda that – we went through this stupid naming ceremony where we put our costume and make-up and most importantly our stupid red noses on, the red nose is fucking sacred to Lucinda, how sad is that, a ping-pong ball painted with nail polish, it's supposed to make us either 'in clown' (red nose on, breathing blocked, snot collecting in bottom of ping-pong ball) or 'out of clown' (red nose around neck on elastic, big creases across cheeks where elastic has been pulling too tight). Anyway the naming ceremony goes like this, you put all your clown stuff on, including, finally, the nose, and you're supposed to have this big spontaneous moment where suddenly your inner clown is released and bingo, you've taken on its personality and given it a name. And Bingo is about the standard of most of the names these retards picked. Bingo, Bungo, Pongo, Ginger. And I'm sitting there waiting for my turn, waiting for my clown to reveal himself and all I can think is how much I want my clown to be called Cunt. Cunt the Clown, ha ha. But I realize this would be going too far, even for me, Lucinda'll probably cark it or something, so when I get up in front of all those other bozos I just say the first word I thought of, which was Dog. So now I'm Dog the Clown. Rough, rough.

And I'm sitting there in my stupid clown pyjamas with my idiot clown nose on and fat Ginger's just sat down and some other moron is rubbing her back, like, oh, thank you, Ginger, that was so cool, and Lucinda the bitch picks me. I mean, I know I've got to do it, I can't get out of it, it's what this fucking course is all about, doing things you don't want to, it's like the fucking army. When are they going to give us the class in cigarette smoking for Christ's sake? Or scowling? Or swinging a mean right hook? That's all Brando and Dean ever did and thank Jesus too, none of this pussy touchy feely shit. But not me, not Barking Billy here, I've got to Discover My Clown.

So I stand up. I walk to the middle of the room in front of the class. My mind's a blank. How can I make something up? I can't think of anything. What am I supposed to do? What is my clown supposed to be? I just stand there and look out into the air and I can't think of anything. Then I remember my name is Dog and so I get down on my hands and knees and start growling. I look at the class, their eyes are on the same level as mine, and I growl at them a bit more. I give them a really good snarl, then I start snapping my teeth. Some of them are frightened, I can see it. Ginger is holding the hand of the girl next to her and shaking her head. I move towards her, slowly, growling. I think about letting out a big drool, a big slobbery drool all over Ginger's feet, and it cracks me up. I start laughing, it all seems so fucking stupid, I just start giggling really bad and I can't stop. I hear Lucinda saying,

—Keep in the moment, Dog, stay in the moment, though her voice sounds kind of quivery and I get the feeling she doesn't much like where the moment is going. It doesn't seem funny any more and I stand up. I look at her and I tell it to her straight.

—Lucinda, why do you think so many psychos dress up as clowns?

—Dog, your nose is on.

—My name's Billy and I don't care if my fucking nose is on or not. It's just a fucking ping-pong ball, Lucinda, it's not a magic wand.

—Dog, in my class when the nose is on, the clown is on. Now if you want to take the nose off that's fine.

—No, I say. —I don't think I do want to take the nose off. Did you ever see that film with Brian Dennehy in it, Lucinda? Any of you guys?

Some of the class have taken their noses off, some of them are just sitting there nodding. They're all watching me. It feels great. The girl next to Ginger starts crying.

—He was a fucking psycho, Lucinda. He was a clown who used to fuck young boys and then kill them. How do you feel about that, Lucinda? Do you think he should have taken his nose off first? Huh?

—Billy, you are poisoning the air in my class, says Lucinda. She's shaking and her nostrils are totally white. I've never seen her like this, not even the time in the group improvisation when I made everyone kiss my feet – clowns are so gullible.

She holds the door open. —Please leave.

—I will be leaving this stupid fucking idiot class, Lucinda, you dumb cunt, I tell her with my nose still on, enjoying every minute of this, —and I will not be coming back.

Then I bow to the rest of the class, give Lucinda the finger, and walk out the door. I can hear the shocked silence behind me. I was waiting to do this for a long time.

I'm in the bathroom trying to get all the white crap off my face when the Drama Centre Administrator comes in. He tells me I've upset not only Lucinda but several of the other students as well, and it won't be possible for me to continue my term here. I don't say anything, I just keep washing my face, and when he says —Billy? Do you have anything to say? I flick water in his eyes and growl like Dog. He leaves pretty quickly. And I'm thinking that the only thing that pisses me off is, now I won't get a refund on my fee.

So I get home thinking, fuck, now what am I going to do, I'll have to go and sign on tomorrow, and there's a message to call my mother. I call her and she tells me that my sister, my stupid dumb beautiful fuck-up sister, has decided to accuse the whole family of involving her in a child molestation cult from the age of three to eleven. Which considering that I'm two years younger than she is, is pretty interesting.

—

I'm in a café drinking a coffee, surprise surprise, when all of a sudden I realize the two girls at the next table are talking about me. I don't know how I know, something in me just picks it up, I'm scanning the paper, not really reading it, when I hear—

—You know I see that guy around all the time.

—Which one?

—Just there.

They're talking all low and whispery. I pretend I can't hear, pretend to be engrossed in some stupid sports page, as if.

—I've seen him around so much, and you know what?

—What?

—I've never once, ever, seen him in the company of anyone else. He is always on his own.

The girl says this like it's the weirdest thing in the world. It really pisses me off. Who the fuck is she, to watch me and decide I'm some loner freak? Who does the bitch think she is? I put my paper down and look at her. She's looking at her friend, who's looking at me. Her friend says something and the girl turns and looks at me. She looks embarrassed. I hold her gaze until she looks away. I look at the friend and she looks away too. Dumb bitches. I go back to my paper. When I've finished my coffee I walk past their table on my way out. I stop by her chair, put my hand on her shoulder and smile.

—See you, I say, like we're old buddies.

She just about jumps out of her skin, then she laughs.

—See you, she says.

It wasn't what I was expecting. I don't know, I don't know anything about her. The friend looks like an idiot, but the girl who thinks I'm a freak – she looks kind of nice. Once I'm out of the café I look back through the window to see if she's looking at me.

—

And so now my sister's coming over. God knows what this crazy shit's about. Satanic ritual abuse? My family? Don't make me laugh. What it is, is she'll have been seeing some asshole shrink who wants to keep the money coming in for a few more sessions, and they'll have said, so, Carol, do you ever think you might have been . . . abused? And my sister's such a sucker, she's gorgeous but she's a total waster, she'll go, yeah, hey, now that you mention it – I really think I might have been forced to eat live babies while being raped by a pig down at our local church on Thursday nights. I mean, it's hard to understand, but it's just her – she's got several screws loose. She's been anorexic since before it was fashionable and she likes sex way too much. I'm no prude, but she is constantly getting herself in these really warped situations with guys who are called things like Mario and Luigi and have these horrible long fingernails. My parents are such morons, she's got them totally fooled with her 'harmless fun' act, but not me.

I fall asleep while I'm waiting for Carol and wake up freezing and sore from the floor. I dreamed that my feet were cold and I had to burn my shoes to keep warm. That was the good thing about the Drama Centre – about the only good thing – it got me out of the house in the mornings. Now I'll just sleep for hours, I know it, like before, and my dreams'll start seeming more real than my waking time. Maybe they are, anyway, who's to say. Let's face it, that Drama Centre was worse than any nightmare I could have dreamt up anyway. Fuck who needs them. I can still be an actor. I can still be anything.

—

—I'm a survivor, Billy, says Carol, all shaky and thin.

—Of what, Carol, I say, —Auschwitz? Because that's what you look like.

—This is real, Billy. You don't know how hard it is. I'm frightened for you.

She's chain-smoking and ashing all over the floor, it's not like I'm houseproud but she could be reasonable. She helps herself to some more Scotch. First thing she told me was, she's not pressing charges – yet. Her bitch shrink wants her to 'as part of the healing process', yeah, right, healing whose bank account? But Carol's toying with the idea of forgiveness first. Good one. Thing is, she knows there's no money to be got at anyway, something Ms Freud obviously hasn't been told.

—Then how come I don't remember any of this? I say to her. —Tell me why you can have so-called flashbacks of burning crosses and purple hoods and all that blood and shit, and I don't?

—You're blocking, that's all.

—Oh, come on, Carol, you're sounding like one of my

drama teachers for Jesus' sake. How can I be blocking anything that isn't there?

—Don't you think there's something creepy about Mum and Dad? Don't you get creepy vibes when you go there? To that house? She's really letting herself freak now, barely keeping her hands still enough to get the drink to her mouth.

—Of course they're creepy, I say, and I can't help laughing, —they're total shitheads, Dad's some moron asshole and Mum's a whinging cunt, it doesn't make them the High Priest and Priestess of Beelzebub. They're just your average parental creeps, Carol, nothing more or less.

I'm getting a little bit pissed off by now, Carol's drinking all my Scotch and I'm surprised she's bothering to keep this bullshit act going for so long.

—I was abused and I know it, she says, sniffing. —Marian said people would try and deny my reality—

—Who's Marian? Your shrink?

Carol nods.

—She's a sick bitch, Carol, face it. What kind of pervert is she to put these things into your head?

—She didn't put anything in there! Carol stands up and just about screams it at me. —It's all here! Here, here, here!

She starts banging her head with her fists and crying. Holy Jesus, I wasn't prepared for this. I'm finding it a bit spooky, I've got to admit.

—I'm sorry, I say, —fuck, Carol—

—Don't say that word! she screeches, —don't say it, you don't know what it means, you're a pawn, Billy, a victim, a henchman!

I try and put my arm around her but she throws me off. She goes and slumps down in the corner, crying. I pour myself some Scotch. Fuck, I need it. This is crazy. This is just some crazy shit.

—Carol . . .

I stop. I don't say anything. We sit in silence for a while, then she gets up and straightens herself and lights her last cigarette, always a sign she's going to leave.

—God, Billy, do you have to have all those pictures of James Dean all over the place? Don't you get sick of them? Why don't you ever open a window?

I don't even answer this. About the only real fight we ever had was when she tried to tell me James Dean was a fag. Bull fucking shit.

—Could I borrow some money? I feel bad asking her, especially now, but God knows Mario or Luigi or whoever that greasy bastard is gives her enough to play with. It's not like she spends it on food. She sighs, and takes a twenty out of her pocket.

—Why don't you get a job?

—Drama Centre. No point telling her I quit. —Thanks.

—When did you last have a job, Billy?

—Don't start with me.

She comes over to me and kisses me on the lips.

—Keep your pretty head low, she says.

I start to say something but she's gone.

—

I am just waiting for the day when she sticks her tongue in my mouth during her goodbye kiss. I fucking dream about that day, her soft mouth and her wet tongue and her skinny legs, treating me like she used to when we were too young to know better. One day it's got to happen but it better be soon, at this rate the next place I'll be visiting Carol is the loony bin. In the meantime it's just me and my fantasies, fucking around and around in my head.

—

—You're tearing me apart.
   That's James Dean, in East of Eden.
   —You're tearing me apart.
   I watch it all weekend.

—

And it's weird, I guess it's a coincidence, I'm in the same café and there's that girl again, the one who thinks I'm some strange-o lone wolf. She's on her own this time, which is kind of a neat twist. The place is packed so I've got a good excuse when I ask to share her table. She looks at me in that way like she's trying to pretend I'm just another person, she's never seen me before. But I know and she knows and she knows I know. I watch her while she's reading her book. She doesn't like this. Finally she cracks.
   —Is there something wrong?
   —No, I say, —you look familiar, that's all.
   She's really hating this. She glances around to see if there's another table free. Bad luck, babe, you're stuck with me.

—I don't think I know you, she says slowly, then goes back to her book, really cool like she's got everything sussed, I don't faze her. But I can see her eyes and they're glued to the same words, she's not reading anything, this book thing's not going anywhere.

—My name's Billy, I say. —I do have a name.

She puts her book down and looks me in the eye. I have to say I admire her for this. I can tell she's weighing it up, talk to the freak or chicken out.

—I'm Karen.

I like a girl who can rise to a challenge. Karen, that's nice. She's not as skinny as Carol but there's a similarity there.

—Hi, Karen, I say, and smile. —Bye, Karen.

And I leave her there, keep her guessing, thinking any time I want I can go back to this café and she'll be there, it's fine, she's here for me now.

—

There are about eight messages from my mother. On the last three of them, she's crying. This is probably the exact response that Carol's after – she was always better at achieving it than me. I'm pissed off with my mother for taking this whole thing so seriously – can't she just get a life? Dad'll be on her back, what did you do wrong, you're a useless mother, why do your children hate you? Convenient memory loss on his part.

—

Then this was the week we would have started rehearsing our final production from the drama course. Fucking Lucinda. They'll be doing some horror, some crap expressionist thing with everyone in whiteface. Now *Streetcar* – if they were doing that, I'd spit. I practise in the mirror – Stella! Stella! I've got it down. I wish I was living in hot sweaty New Orleans instead of this dumb fuck cold town. Nothing's happening, nothing's happening, nothing's happening. Nothing's happening.

—

I have this dream where I'm in a cupboard with Carol. We're kids, just young, and we're in this cupboard together and I really like it, I feel good, you know, here I am and I've got Carol all to myself and it's kind of fun in the dark. But then I get the idea that we're stuck here, we can't get out, and I start to get scared. I start crying, like a real baby, and I'm so scared and I want whoever put us in here to let us out now, I'm fucking panicking, shit, then Carol isn't Carol anymore, she's fucking Lucinda and she's laughing and laughing and she's got this big clown mouth laughing and laughing and I wake up shit scared, breathing fast, clammy, with my blankets all twisted around me. This has got to be a joke.

Darling Billy (this is what the letter says)
    You've always been the only one who understands me, the only one I can trust. I love you. But I can't take you

down this road with me. Some scary stuff's going to come
up and the best thing is to leave you out of it. Marian says I
need to do this on my own. I'm going away for a bit to work
out exactly what I want to do. I don't know if everything
will be all right or not. Just please take care of yourself. I
can't tell you not to talk to them but it'll be better if you
don't.

I know you probably think this is part of my victim act
but I'm not going to be a victim of this, Billy, I'm a survivor,
I promise. Be one too.
love Carol.


She is such a drama queen. Who's them? She must mean
Mum and Dad. This is getting ridiculous. I could kill her
fucking shrink.

—

So, because there seems less and less to do with my days and
I've got to get out of the house so I don't have to hear my
mother shrieking on the answer machine for the thirty-
seventh time, I go to the café. I walk up and down the street
outside it first, looking in, trying to see if Karen's there. It
gets too miserable to stay outside so I go in, I can't see her
anywhere but I get a coffee anyway, read Carol's letter over
and over, imagine Marian standing behind her while she
writes it, talking that stupid shrink-speak – you can do it,
Carol, this is empowering, visualize yourself in a safe
environment – Carol wouldn't know a fucking safe environment if she was on a witness protection programme. Witless

protection is what she needs. I hate shrinks, I hate them, especially fucking losers like Marian who can't stop messing with other people's lives. The one time I saw a shrink – my father forced me, he thought I was a fag and I didn't bother telling him otherwise – she tried to get me to talk to a chair. Fuck that shit. Pretend the chair is your father, she told me, now is there anything you want to say to him? Yeah, Dad, get off all fours, I said, which OK isn't that funny, but she got really pissed off. Don't you think you should overcome your fear of embarrassment? she said. Oh, I said, is that what I'm here to overcome? Silly me, I thought it was my fear of fucking women that we were working through here, bitch, and by the way have you got teeth up there under that tweed skirt? Bet you do. She kicked me out, of course, told me I was a very sick boy and needed help that she wasn't qualified to give. Funny how people think they can handle anything until you get them where they live. At least it got my fat fuck father off my case.

The waitress is looking at me weird. What the fuck's the matter?

It's not as if I don't have any friends anyway. I could have friends if I wanted, it's just the losers that inhabit this town aren't worth my time and effort. Carol's my friend. I mean, she is my sister, too, but it goes beyond that. Carol would be my friend even if we were raised in different families. And from everything she's saying now, it looks like that might be the way it was. It's not as if I never had a girlfriend either. I did have a girlfriend at high school, which seems to me about the only time in your life when it matters whether or not you have one. Mum and Dad didn't know about her because there was no need for them to know, they only would've wanted to meet her and that would have been a force fucking ten disaster. There wasn't anything wrong with her but they would have found something. She's not our religion, Billy, she's too young, Billy, she's got dirty eyes and a dirty mouth, Billy. She did too. That was about all we bothered with really, that and wandering through the hills behind school looking for other people's roaches to smoke. She used to hassle me, tell me I was just a mixed-up middle-class boy with nothing to do. Lucy, Lucy. Juicy Luce. Her family moved town. I got a couple of letters and then nothing. I wonder if I could find her now. She's probably fat with three kids on the dole.

Carol's first boyfriend, though – I do remember him. The first one that mattered. I was fourteen, she was sixteen. I was sick with jealousy. It wouldn't have mattered so much if I'd at least liked him – but fuck he was a pretentious cunt. Drove a VW Beetle that he thought was really cool – had some idiot name for it – and used to come round and call me pal while Carol stuck her diaphragm in in the bathroom. It was so unfair, he was such a prick, and at night I had to lie in bed listening to them get one last poke in outside Carol's bedroom window. She used to moan and carry on, not too loud in case Mum and Dad heard, but enough to make him think he was the hottest thing in baggy trousers. Sometimes she'd climb in my window – I never knew if it was by mistake, or she was drunk, or what – and I could smell her all drink and sex and cigarettes. Once I didn't pretend to stay asleep and she sat on my bed and talked. I even managed to choke my pride and asked what it was like. I could see her roll her eyes in the dimness and she said, Oh – you know, Billy – everything it's cracked up to be. But her voice was flat and hollow. And after Baggy Trousers there was Jeff and he was even worse, and after Jeff there was another and another until she met Mario or Luigi and he introduced her to all his friends and she stopped limiting herself to just one at a time.

When I get home from the café I see my mother's car parked outside my building. Shit. There's got to be a way of avoiding this. There is. I turn around, like somebody pretending they've forgotten something so it doesn't look as if they've got lost or gone the wrong way, and walk down to the river. It's the usual scene of scuzzy tramps and teenage petrol sniffers, only tonight I don't accept anyone's offer of a mouthful of brown muck. I sit on a broken concrete post, my arse getting colder as the night gets darker, and think about Marlon. How could you get so fat and gross, Marlon? How could you start wearing kaftans and that stupid ponytail? God, he used to be so beautiful. I don't know, that better-to-burn-out stuff seems to make sense when I think about him. But then I look over at one group of kids standing right down by the river, passing a plastic bag between them and it gives me the shits. They're not going down in a blaze of glory. They're not going anywhere. They'll probably never even leave this dumbass place. Dumb. Ass.

—

Some days go by and I don't hear any more from Carol. I
don't hear any more from my mother either, thank Christ.
She's probably locked herself in her room and praying her
guts out. It's only in the gap of their silence that I wonder
why I haven't heard anything from my father about this. I'd
have thought he'd be the first on my case, asking what this
nonsense was all about, did I put Carol up to it, push me
around the room a little bit, then try and hold my hand and
make me ask forgiveness from the Lord for being such a
little shit. When I imagine this I realize how lucky I am that
he's not around hounding me. I make a decision not to pick
up the phone or answer the door. But nobody rings and
nobody knocks. Why isn't he calling me? It seems like a
bad tactic, like an admission of something. There's no way
I believe that weirdo sex-on-the-altar-candles-and-bones
rubbish that Carol's claiming to remember, but maybe there
was something else. Maybe there was something that just
went on with her.

—

I'm in town standing in the street just outside the café,
wondering whether or not to go in, when the door opens
and she just about walks into me.

    —Karen, I say. —Hi.

    She looks at me blank and then I see her remember who
I am.

    —Hi, she says. She looks over her shoulder and I hope
that idiot friend of hers isn't coming out behind her, but

there's no one there. She looks at her watch. She starts
walking and I walk with her.

—What are you up to? I say.

—Oh, nothing much. I'm just going to visit a friend.

She's trying to brush me off. How can I stop her? I really
want to talk to her, to get to know her properly. She looks
like she'd be good to talk to, like she's different from the
other stupid schmucks around here, like she'd understand
how things are.

—Um, Karen—. She's gotten a few steps ahead of me
down the street and she stops and turns round.

—Yes? and there's anger and impatience in her voice,
fuck, she just thinks I'm a weirdo twister, how am I going to
get through to her, how can I make her see?

—Do you want to, um . . . ?

—What, she says, and she's biting her tongue I can tell,
she's thinking why is this fuckwit talking to me in the street,
I don't even know him, why did I tell him my name?

Fuck, I think. Piss. —Nothing, I say, and she makes a
dismissive half-wave with her hand and keeps on walking. I
stand there for a while. It's after five and the street's filling
up with people leaving work. I can still see her up by the
movie complex and without really thinking about it I start
to follow her.

—

I was careful. I sat on the same bus as her and she didn't
even see me. I got off when she did and stood around the

corner while she went to the dairy. I watched her come out
with the paper and a carton of milk and I saw her go across
the road and into her house. I know where she lives.

—

I'm on my way to the café again, to see if she's there – I'm
not going to talk to her this time, just want to see her – and
I hear someone calling my name.

—Billy! Hi!

It's the fat girl from the Drama Centre. She's running
over the road towards me. She just about gets hit by a car,
the fat slob idiot – and here she is, grinning at me like a
maniac.

—How are you? like we're bosom buddies. I give her a
look of disgust but it washes right over her fat pink face.
She's so enthusiastic, what's she got to be enthusiastic
about?

—Everyone's been wondering how you are, what happened to you – we had a couple of group meetings so we
could all work through what you did in class that day, but I
think we've all come to terms with it. Oh, it's so good to see
you, what are you doing? The others will be dying to know.
Have you lost weight? You look so thin!

I look at her in amazement. If she doesn't stop gushing
on me I'll puke on her shoes. How can she even ask
somebody else about their weight without wanting to die of
embarrassment? She takes my look for something entirely
different.

—Oh, Billy, you don't need to feel bad about what

happened – I forgive you, I really do, and I know Lucinda
has too. You felt a lot of pressure, anyone could see that,
and clowning is a very big challenge.

I want to laugh. If clowning's a big challenge then standing
in the street listening to this idiot rave is the biggest of them
all. She's the big challenge, stupid Ginger with her fat arms
and her orange hair. She's still going. I can't believe this girl.

—and then, if you're not ready to explore, it can create
an almost aggressive environment, you were only reacting
against that, it's obvious, and now Lucinda's got over her
feelings of inadequacy that she had because she couldn't
reach you – you should come back and see us, Billy, the
production finishes this weekend – come and say hi, just
drop in, we'd all love to know what you're up to now.

I am truly touched. Those creeps. It's taking a lot of effort
not to say anything but if I do there'll be trouble, I know,
and I don't want to destroy Ginge right here in the street.
She squeezes my arm and I'm just about sick, then she looks
deep into my eyes.

—You really have talent, Billy. I really believe that. Don't
give up.

Then – this is the worst part – she kisses my cheek. I rub
it off as she squeezes me again and says, take care. I watch
her fat back and elephant legs bounce down the street in
shock. She's wearing the stupid Drama Centre sweatshirt
with a picture of the sad mask and the happy mask, and
underneath it says, There's method in our madness! Christ.
Thank God I got out of there before I turned into one of
those earnest born-again type crazies. By now I'm too

depressed to go into the café, too depressed to look for Karen. I just go home.

And there it all is again, my flat, the mess, the answer machine with one message – the video shop telling me *Eden* and *Rebel* are weeks late, as if I didn't know. The phone rings and I let the machine pick it up. There's a hesitation after my message, and then someone hangs up. Carol. Damn. Where the fuck is she?

—

I don't leave the flat for a few days, hoping she'll ring again, ordering delivery Chink food and watching Dean until I can do the whole thing myself, backwards. Natalie Wood reminds me of Karen. I think about her, too, remember her street, the bus ride over the bridge to her house, the shabby suburb she lives in, shabby but OK in a not too arty kind of way. I think about her in her house, walking around, taking a bath, talking on the phone. I wonder what she does. I wonder when I'll see her again. Then one afternoon I get up, groggy, and there's a letter under the door. The envelope says To Billy from Carol, like it's a note on a Christmas present or something.

Billy. I've spoken to Louise and told her what I want.

It takes me a while to figure out who Louise is, then I realize she's talking about our mother.

She's agreed to come and see Marian with me. We need to talk about this as a family. The idea of even being in the

same room as her scares me, but I know it's something that
has to be done. The only way she will face this is if we talk
about it, and I can only do that with Marian in the room.
I've asked her to bring Ken but I don't know if he'll come.
He's very angry with me and he's a very influential man,
Billy, so be careful. These people are everywhere. You just
don't know.

Her writing's all spindly and shaky. I smell the letter but it
doesn't smell of Carol, just of paper.

> I want you to come too, Billy. It will help you to remember.
> This is the most important thing I've ever asked you to do.
> If you love me, I'll see you there.

And in the envelope is also a card with an address and a
time on it. Tomorrow. I don't like this. I don't like it at
all.

I try to write a letter to Karen but it's no good. Can't say
what I feel. I end up just writing her name out, with mine,
over and over and over again. We will be together, soon. It's
nearly the right time. We're going to save each other from
this shit-heap.

—

So this is as far down as it's gone – further than I could have
imagined was possible – and now here I am. God, it's like I
can pinpoint everything back to that damn fuck drama class,
when something gave somewhere and the stench really

started to seep in. I can't decide what to do. I get right up to the building where Carol's shrink works without knowing if I'm going in or not. I spent a lot of last night imagining the scene, and it always took place in a high brick building with wooden-floored offices inside. I'd stand by the window looking out, while Carol and our parents threw allegations and insults at each other. Finally I'd turn around, give Marian and Louise and Ken a withering look of disgust, take Carol by the hand and lead her out with me, into my car which is waiting to take us to some big city, where we live in freedom without any bullshit.

But now I'm here in front of it, and it's a low-slung prefab-type building, you can imagine, cork notice-boards with sad old 'does anyone want to buy some puppies', or 'youthlink – meet interesting young people' messages on them. And retards shuffling around in slippers, twitching, and women like Lucinda making cups of herbal tea and being patronizing. It makes me laugh to think of my parents stuck in there, sitting in a circle with Carol and her stupid shrink. It makes me feel sick, too. Dad'll probably have a fucking stroke. I didn't have to leave the army you know, he'll shout, again – I did it for my family, I could have been a Major – yeah, right, Dad, you already are, Major Asshole. And your lovely wife, Mrs Asshole. Oh, I'm tired of this. Standing outside this building feels familiar to me, like standing outside buildings is something I've done all my life. I smoke half a pack of cigarettes I've bought specially for the occasion, and I leave.

I feel like an asshole for ditching Carol like this, but fuck.

She can't seriously expect me to go through with it. It's not even so much having to listen to all the crap Marian's going to talk, or to Carol reeling off these fantasy atrocities of hers, or my father clearing his throat and my mother crying softly. It's the thought of all the stuff they'll want to dredge up, the shit they'll want to sift through, trying to prove they were perfect parents, trying to prove their innocence. And Dad might be angry but Carol's angry too, angry and out for some revenge. I don't want to have to hear it.

I wander around for a bit, feeling as if I'm at the end of something. I don't know what it is but not going into that building feels like more than I know. I think about going back to my flat but I don't want to do that. I don't want to watch those vidoes again, I don't want to sleep, I don't want to think about what I'm going to do tomorrow. What am I going to do tomorrow? I can't think of anything I would want to do.

I see a bus coming and I get on it. It goes across the bridge. It's a sign. All in the timing. Karen. There's got to be a way of getting through to her. I know I could talk to her, try and explain, and she'd listen to me. I think if she got to know me she'd like me, too. I'm sure she would. Here's her stop. I get off and remember the way to her house. I'm just going to stand outside it and look at it, imagine her, maybe pretend to bump into her when she gets home. Maybe she already is home. I walk up to the door and knock, afraid she's going to answer it, afraid she's not going to answer it. I lean my head against the cold wood of the door. Nobody comes. I go around the side of the house and see what must be the bathroom window. I take the louvres out and climb in.

—

It smells nice in here, in Karen's house, clean and nice. I walk around looking at her things, posters of ethnic-looking prints, rugs, old pots and shit. She's kind of a hippy, I guess. Well, that's okay. There's not much in the fridge. Maybe she doesn't look after herself properly. I eat some leftover rice but it's cold and hard. I find her room. By her bed there's a table with photographs on it. Karen by the Taj Mahal, Karen with her arms around a dog, Karen with some idiot-looking guy. That friend of hers from the café's there too. I rip a bit out of the picture so the guy's not in it any more. That's better. I lie on the bed for a bit. Smell the pillow. Girl smell. Mustn't fall asleep. There's a scarf draped over the foot of the bed. I pick it up and run it through my fingers. Soft. Wrap it round my hand for later.

I open her wardrobe door. There's the skirt she was wearing the first day I saw her, and the coat she had on when I followed her home. They smell sort of musty like hippies' clothes smell, love oil or whatever that crap is they use. We can talk when she gets home, talk, then maybe go to a movie or something, or go to my place and watch my videos. I wouldn't mind seeing them with her. And when Carol's better she can meet Karen and maybe we could all go away somewhere together. A big city, yeah, or the other side of the world even. In a car. The three of us. That'd be good.

*barking*

I climb into Karen's wardrobe and shove her shoes in the corner so I can sit down on her floor. I pull the door closed so it's dark. Sometimes I wonder if I've been a fool with my life. But right now this is all I want to do, sit here in Karen's wardrobe in the dark, bits of hard rice in the side of my mouth, Karen's clothes brushing against my face. Waiting for her to come and find me.

# the shared experience

These are her options.

1. Drive away. The keys are in the ignition. He's in the back of a long queue waiting to pay for the petrol. The car's an expensive one. She could get a lot of money for it. Quietly open her door, take the petrol pump out of the car, get in the driver's side and take off with a full tank. Drive as far as she can, to the nearest port. Sell the car to someone who doesn't want to see the papers. Get on a boat. Disappear.
2. Stay in the car. Go to the hotel. Feign exhaustion. Order food up to her room, have a bath, go to bed alone.
3. Stay in the car. Go to the hotel. Cross the line that's been waiting to be crossed all day. Become the sort of woman who sleeps with her boss.

He comes back to the car, folding the receipt into his wallet. She sits politely in the passenger seat, hands crossed in her lap. Say goodbye to Option 1.

He starts the car and pulls out into the traffic. He jerks his seatbelt over his shoulder. The buckle won't do up.

—Can you?

She twists in her seat and tries to jam the buckle into the thing it's supposed to jam into. His left hand moves over, as if to help. It's big and dry and covers both of her hands. She feels the flush starting at her throat and moving round to the back of her neck. She has a tendency to go blotchy when embarrassed. She hopes he doesn't notice. The buckle finally clicks into place and he moves his hand back to the steering wheel. She turns round to face front and presses the button to unwind her window. Pushing her sunglasses up on her nose, she sneaks a look at his hands, their casual touch on the wheel. Big hands. Big hands with a big gold wedding ring on one of them. When she went to America she wore a ring on her wedding finger, a cheap imitation number she'd picked up from a street stall. Her sister told her it was bad luck, that if you wore a ring on that finger without being married, it meant you never would be. Her sister's authority on luck was questionable, as she was married at the time to a man called Dwayne who spent all his money on gambling and had no sense of humour. This seemed like a fate far worse than spinsterhood, but she didn't say so to her sister. The fake American wedding ring seems ridiculous now, a flimsy attempt to shield herself from physical or emotional danger. She laughs.

—What's funny?

She can't tell him she's thinking about wedding rings.

—Nothing.

—You're a strange one.

Why did men feel compelled to say things like that to her? Really and truly. What a horrible thing to say. You're a strange one – it's not the kind of thing you'd ever say to someone you considered an equal, is it? Well, so, he's never going to leave his wife for her. It doesn't mean Option 3 couldn't still happen.

He clears his throat. —Do you mind if I put a tape on?

—No.

This'll be it. If it's *Eric Clapton Unplugged* she's definitely not going to bed with him. In fact the list of tapes that would put her off him is potentially endless. *Yodelling Favourites. Ravel's Bolero. Twenty Big Band Hits.* Anything played by Kenny Gee.

—Do you want to find one? They're in the glove box.

Oh shit. Shit shit shit. This way it's her own taste on the line – at least, her choice of his selection. She opens the glove box and yes, it's her worst nightmare. Next to the maps and a tube of toothpaste (toothpaste?) are five or six tapes of classical music. Does it have to be this way? She knows next to nothing about classical music. It occupies the same place in her head as wine lists, or the inside of car engines. Things she can't concentrate on long enough to ever figure out. OK, don't panic, breathe. What have we got here? Mozart, Mozart, Haydn, Beethoven, Handel. Mozart's nice, isn't he? What's the difference between Haydn and Handel? Opus? What does that even mean? She pulls out a tape at random. Beethoven. The deaf guy. OK then, here we go.

Big dark booming notes bounce around the car.

—Jesus, says her boss. —That's a bit grim.

—Yeah, sorry, she says, and presses stop. The tape won't eject and she pushes and pushes the button desperately till it pops out.

—I don't know what that tape's doing there, he says. —I haven't heard it in years.

—What one do you want?

—Oh, you choose.

This is starting to feel like a challenge. She grabs one of the Mozart tapes and shoves it in the tape deck. She turns to the window again, hot with embarrassment and anger.

—That's nice, he says, and she feels a bit better. The countryside rolls past and she starts to feel much better. The tape crisis is over, and now they don't have to talk.

They arrive in the town where the meeting is going to be held just as it's getting dark. Standing at the reception desk in the hotel, she is struck by the full force of the romance of the situation. Here they are, checking into a hotel together. Sure, they're getting separate rooms and they're here on business and they're not lying to the receptionist about their last names, but still – anything could happen. She stands just behind her boss while he does the talking with the woman at the desk. He passes her a key. She turns it over and over, feeling the cool outline of its ridges warming up in her hand, the embossed 13F on the tag.

She follows him down the hall, clutching her small weekend bag, trying to take in the old wallpaper and gilt-framed paintings and thick carpets without losing her blasé expression. She could probably count the number of hotels she's stayed in on one hand. She steps into the lift. He presses the button for their floor. The silence in the lift is excruciating. Say something, say something, she tells herself. There must be something to say. The lift stops. They check their keys.

—I think, right . . . and the . . . He could be talking to himself. She pretends not to notice.

Her room is right next to his. They stand in front of their respective doors. She looks at her shoes.

—Have you got everything ready for tomorrow?

—Yes, she says, —I've just got to sort some papers together.

—Mm, yes, I've got a couple of calls I'd better make and then I thought I'd grab a bite. We may as well eat downstairs. Half an hour?

He's inside his room with the door shut before he's finished talking, before she says, OK. She puts her hand to her face and feels how hot it is. She lets herself into her room.

It's small, just a double bed next to a window looking on to the wall of the next building. There's a door leading to a shower cubicle, basin and toilet. She washes her hands and lies down on the bed. Through the wall by her head she can hear him talking. She shuts her eyes and feels a rush of tiredness, and something like nausea. She sits up and blinks, dizzy. There's not enough oxygen in here. She kicks her shoes off, enjoying the thump they make as they hit the floor. When she was a teenager she used to throw her shoes against the wall of her bedroom just to listen to the sound of it.

Should she change for dinner? The clothes she's been

wearing in the car all day feel sticky and gross, but maybe changing would look like she was making too much effort. Perhaps one thing. She decides to keep her skirt and change her top. She takes the papers for tomorrow's meeting out of her bag and spreads them out on the floor. Can't be fucked sorting through them now. Her own company is making her tired. She takes a small bottle of vodka out of her bag and has a couple of mouthfuls. Drinking with inferiors again, she thinks, and laughs. She'd better be careful.

The shower's a dribbly contraption with water that runs only extremely hot or extremely cold. She shivers under it for a minute and gets out. Drying herself, she has an idea. Maybe she shouldn't wear any knickers. Wouldn't it be exciting not to, in a private and slightly scary kind of way? But it would make her even more self-conscious than she already is. She can imagine getting a kick out of it though, feeling powerful and secretive as she toys with her linguine. Though if anything happens between them later, he'll know and he might think she's overly forward. Unless he's the kind of man who likes that. Maybe she'd feel too vulnerable. And then, if nothing does happen, she'll feel like an idiot. Of course, nobody ever needs to know. Option three, Option three, she sings to her reflection in the steamed-up mirror. No. It's stupid. He's her boss, for goodness sake. They've got to work tomorrow. She should be preparing for this meeting instead of fantasizing about his big hands and his pin-striped suit. This is just a power displacement thing. She should want to screw him figuratively, get his job or something, not literally. That's not going to get her anywhere. Besides, he's married. How can she even be considering this? Has she got no scruples at all? She could at least pretend to have a moral dilemma about this. But the only dilemma she's having is whether or not to put on her underwear. Well. That settles it. She puts her clothes back on, including her bra and knickers, and brushes her hair.

There, a nicely presented young woman. Competent, attractive, and desperate. She must be desperate, to have fixated on her boss like this. He is good-looking, there's no doubt about that. But surely she should be looking for someone from her own peer group? Well, it's obvious why she isn't. They're all fatuous, self-obsessed, undirected, confused, emotional retards. Whereas her boss, her managing director – she loves those words! – is nothing like that. He's young for his position – he must be driven, focused. And he's interesting, isn't he, and knowledgeable? She lights a cigarette and sits back down on the bed. So what if he is, and so what if he isn't? She's fascinated by him the same way she's mesmerized in the menswear sections of department stores. She can wander around them for hours, hypnotized by the umbrellas and wallets and canes and gloves. The ties, the hats, the pipes. The smell – no, the *idea* of the smell – of tobacco and leather and shoe polish. She loves it. She loves it all, and she wants to get close to it.

She hears his door shut. Stubs out her cigarette and fans the air. There's a knock on her door. —Coming, she calls. She looks in the mirror. Fuck it, she's going to take a risk. Why the fuck not? She hitches up her skirt, takes off her knickers, and throws them in the corner of the room. There.

She smooths her skirt down and smiles. She's still smiling as she opens the door, looks her managing director straight in the eye, and walks with him down to the restaurant.

—

It probably started at her interview for the job, the first time she shook his hand and smiled her job-interview smile and asked herself what it was he was looking for. But the moment she knew it was there was when she read back a fax she'd typed for him arranging an appointment. Instead of 'if this suits' she'd written 'if his suits'. And as soon as she saw the words she knew they were a sign. If his suits were under her hands. If his suits were pressed against her cheek. If his suits hung in neat rows in his wardrobe. If his suits ever came off. She didn't talk to anyone about this new way she had of looking at him as he sat behind his desk. Watching him on the telephone, or in meetings. Dressing for him every day. When she went drinking with other girls from work she kept her mouth shut as they speculated about his marriage, his past, his private life. Because she worked the closest with him, they accorded her a certain respect, but she could tell that her silence irritated them. She didn't care. She'd get quietly drunk and go home and get more drunk and go to bed and dream, drunkenly, about him.

—

—So, tell me how you find the company, he says.

Her first thought is that he means his company, here tonight, then she realizes.

—Oh, it's good, she says.—I'm enjoying it.

—Not too stuffy?

—Well, they are a bit, she says. —Not everyone, I mean. But, mm. She trails off.

—Yes, well, he says, and laughs. —Wine?

—Yes, please.

—Red all right?

—Sure. You choose, she thinks. Just don't ask me.

—Good. He orders some wine from the sullen waiter. They study the menus.

—This is on the expense account, so have whatever you like. The writing on the menu blurs in front of her eyes. Expense account. Somehow those words expose the tackiness of the situation more than anything so far, the way they conjure up images of travelling salesmen. Men with moustaches. Wife-swapping parties where the car keys get thrown in the swimming pool. The horror, the horror.

—I'll have steak, he tells the waiter, —rare.

He says the word as if it's an announcement, a declaration of his hunger. His carnivorous, bare-fanged hunger. She crosses her legs.

—I'll have the salmon, please.

—With red wine? He raises his eyebrows.

Who is this man, James Bond? —Why not?

Surely this discomfort, this nervousness, this level of tension, means there's something going on? Surely he can feel it too?

—

He takes off his jacket and hangs it over the back of his chair. This is really too much. She's got to stop staring at his hands, their clipped nails, the thick veins running from his knuckles back into his shirtcuffs. The thick brown leather band of his watchstrap, the thick gold band of his wedding ring.

Their wine arrives. She thanks the waiter. He doesn't. She drinks too quickly, eyes down, nearly emptying her glass.

—Cheers. He toasts vaguely in her direction. —Here's to it.

To what, to what, she wants to say. What is this thing? What is this thing called, love? Watch it – she'll make herself laugh again. Can't have that.

—Well, I must say work's a much more pleasant place to be since you've started with us.

Did he really say that? Did she hear him right? She smiles.

—Thanks, she simpers.

—Have you ever been to America?

It's clear to her that the conversation will go wherever he leads it – it won't be appropriate for her to initiate anything. This is probably OK – it's hard to know what she could think of to say anyway.

—Once, she says, and clears her throat. Her voice is coming out funny. —I went to New York, and down to the New Orleans jazz festival. It was great.

—Yeah, it's a pretty exciting place all right. This is off the record – we're thinking of merging with another company there. In New York City actually. I'm going over next month to sound it out.

—Wow. That would be great.

God, is she reduced to this pathetic sort of platitude after everything he says? She makes herself sit up straighter.

—Yes, it could be exciting. As long as they don't swamp us.

—Is it a big company?

—I'd better not say too much. Big enough. He smiles.

She feels like a child being taught how to add with building blocks. This is the big one, see, and this one – that's smaller. Say something intelligent, she tells herself, furious.

—Would there be a staffing merge as well?

He raises his eyebrows at her. —You mean, is there a chance for free trips to the States?

She goes bright red, pulls her napkin onto her lap and twists it hard. —No, that's not—.

He laughs. —I'm teasing. There may be the odd swap – I'm looking into all of that.

She feels as if she's had a sense of humour bypass. Maybe she's just too uptight to get a joke any more.

The restaurant begins to fill with other diners. Old people mostly, the odd lone businessman. What are they thinking of the two of them? What do they look like together? She hopes they look like a glamorous couple. They do suit each other, she's sure of that. She wonders what his wife looks like. She imagines blonde and gorgeous. This is daunting, but at least picture-perfect and unreal.

The salmon comes complete with bones. So unfair. She drops her fork. Did that have to happen? It's an effort to stay on her chair as she slides down to retrieve it. She's just

lifting it back up to the table when the waiter brings her a
new one. Red again. Blotch Girl. Lovely. Her boss eats like
a guy, which is reassuring she supposes – he seems
completely unselfconscious and in control. Since the fork
incident the table has become an obstacle course to her –
everything there only to be knocked over, or spilt, or hit
against something else with a loud and resonant ping.

They talk about travel – he's done a lot, she very little.
And opera – the same. And sailing – that too. She begins to
wonder if there is a topic she knows anything about. Asks
him if he likes going to the movies. It sounds like a come-
on, she knows it even as she's saying it, lets her voice die
away, her sentence unfinished.

—Are you all right there?

—Yes, she smiles brightly, —fine. Pull yourself together,
she thinks. At the same time she thinks it's unfair of him to
draw attention to her nervousness. She's supposed to be
nervous, isn't she? They both know what's in the air, on the
agenda, up for grabs. Of course she's bloody nervous.
Getting angry has a calming effect. She tackles her salmon
again with renewed confidence. Smiles flirtatiously at the
waiter when he pours her more wine. Hopes her boss
notices. He doesn't. Too busy tucking into his steak. Zoltar,
Ruler of the Universe. It's so easy for men.

They somehow muddle through dinner. Her most
hopeful moment is when he orders a second bottle of wine.
Once their plates have been cleared there is a long silence.
All she can think of is touching him. She keeps her eyes
down, for safety. What if she made a move? Just reached

her hand over to his. She experimentally probes under the
table with her foot. Nothing. His feet must be tucked under
his chair. Then he leans back, stretches his legs out, and a
foot collides with hers. She makes herself keep her foot
there. It's a light contact but it's something. Risks a glance
at him. He's looking at her. Oh boy, oh boy. She feels giddy.
Drunk. Smiles. Looks away. Smiles again. Looks back. He
raises his eyebrows. She's entranced by his face, his eyes, his
jaw, his mouth. Wants to kiss him. Feels immobile. Opens
her mouth to say something. Has no words. Closes it again.

—Didn't you do something funny at university? he asks.
—Horticulture or something?

She nods, bewildered. She must have mentioned it at
work. —A couple of papers.

—I should introduce you to my wife, he says. —She's a
very keen gardener.

Jesus, that was out of left field. She manages a smile.
—Oh really.

—Yes. We have a beautiful garden.

What is he raving about? —Excuse me a minute, she says.

She heads towards the bathroom and at the last minute
veers off towards the lifts. She falls into one, back into the
corner, mouth open, head throbbing. Turns to face herself
in the mirrored wall. Christ. Her lipstick's all eaten off. At
least she hasn't got food in her teeth. She staggers to her
room, jabs at the lock with her key, gets in, retrieves her
knickers from their landing place by the waste-paper basket,
drags them on, falling back on her bed in the process – pulls

herself up, smears more lipstick on and goes back down to the restaurant.

—Are you OK?

—Yes, thanks, she says. How long has she been gone from the table? It felt like seconds but maybe it was unnaturally long. She dabs at the corners of her mouth, hoping he'll attribute her absence to bulimia. She shifts in her chair, feeling happier now that she's fully clothed, feeling stronger.

He pours out the last of the wine. Coughs. Says, —Do you mind if I smoke?

—Not at all, she says with relief. At last she can light up herself. He's not going to pull out a cigar is he? No. Thank God. He passes her the lighter. Now is her chance. She lets her fingers brush against his. They look at each other. She can feel the pulse knocking in the base of her throat. Don't blotch, she tells herself, just don't. She lights her cigarette with trembling hands. Light-headed. Feels queasy, almost. That salmon was too rich.

—We must get you on some more interesting projects, he says. —You're a bright girl.

Oh, please, she thinks. —That'd be good.

Doesn't want to talk about work. Doesn't want to talk at all. The waiter comes over, asks if they'd like anything else.

—Cognac? he asks her.

What's the right answer? Yes, stay and have more to drink, or no, go straight to his room? They are going to his room, aren't they? This can't end in nothing. She tries to look noncommittal.

—Two cognacs, he says to the waiter.

And two become four, and four become six. Blurry. Slurring words. A lot of cigarettes. Somewhere between the second and third cognac he reaches under the table and puts his hand on her knee. She's too drunk to blush any more. Blinks slowly. Puts her hand on his hand. Moves her fingers over it, tries to ignore the fucking wedding ring. Just avoids that part of the hand, the way you avoid touching a pimple on someone's back, or a coldsore on their mouth. Watching his two faces, she has to keep herself from squinting in an attempt to bring him into focus.

The waiter hovers. He doesn't even look up.

—Could we have the bill, please.

He slides his hand out from between her hand and her knee, finds his wallet. Takes out a card, puts it on the table.

—What do you think? he says.

She smiles. —What do you think?

—I asked first.

—I think . . . She lights another cigarette, stalling. The waiter brings the receipt back and he signs it.

—I think I'm drunk. The words don't seem as gauche and uncharming to her now as they will when she remembers them later. If she remembers them.

He smiles. —So am I. Shall we go?

Standing up is a bit tricky. She follows him out through the restaurant like an air hostess, steadying herself on the backs of chairs as she passes. Things begin to fragment here. Flashes of consciousness, moments of blankness. It's as if a light somewhere is being turned on and off at random.

Through the reception area. Slippery floor. Don't slip on the floor. The lift. He kisses her in the lift. She feels tired. The awkwardness of standing outside his door while he tries to find his key.

In his room. They're both in his room. It's dark. What if she throws up? He's unlacing his shoes, unbuttoning his shirt. Isn't she supposed to be doing that for him? Come here, he says, and she sits gingerly on the bed next to him. Did she fall over on the way up here? Her knee hurts. He kisses her. She can smell the aftershave smell of him, and smoke. Then they're, you know, fooling around. She feels very uncoordinated. It's kind of nice though. In a far-off sort of a way. Soon it's all happening, the clothes are off, the sheets are off, she's in an out-of-town hotel room doing it with her boss. Oh boy. Shouldn't there be a condom here somewhere? Oh. There is already. She must have missed that bit. How embarrassing. She must have blacked out because a few minutes later she has a sense of time passing and he's still there on top of her, grinding away. This is excruciating. She makes an effort to wake up and get into it. A brief effort. Why is she so detached? Oh come on, come on, get it over with. This seems like it's been going on forever.

It does go on forever, and then it stops. She lies there thinking about her room, thinking she should go back to it. The energy involved in dragging herself out of bed and running to her room with her bundle of clothes seems impossible. She'll just lie here a little bit more. Just a little bit, then she'll go. Her mouth is dry. She's vaguely aware of her boss next to her in the bed, naked, hairy, snoring. How can she ever go back to work for him now? Yuck. As she falls into a stupor, the thought passes through her mind that if he brought condoms, then he must have had some idea of something.

Somewhere in her coma she hears the phone ringing. A light snaps on. Her boss sits bolt upright. He grabs the phone. Doesn't look at her.

—Yes? Hello?

She can hear a woman's voice, faintly, and a child crying, less faintly.

—All right, put her on. Darling? It's Daddy. Hello. Was it a bad dream?

This seems like an opportune moment to leave. Keeping her head down, she grabs her clothes and keys from the floor where they're all jumbled in with his. Remembers to get her earrings from the table – a mistake she's made before, losing jewellery – though she has no memory of taking these off. She shuts the door behind her, not looking back at him, feeling like shit.

Now here she is in the hallway with no clothes on. A nightmare made real. Which door is hers? Her eyes can't focus enough to read the letters. Oh bugger, these aren't her room keys. They're his fucking car keys. Oh Christ. Why her? Why? She performs a crouching half-run up and down the hall, checking for any sign of life. Shivering, she knocks lightly on his door. No answer. She can hear him still talking on the phone. Did he hear her knock? – maybe not. But it's so unbearable to have to make a noise. She takes a deep breath and knocks again, slightly louder. This is hell. People go to the theatre to laugh at things like this. A fucking farce. Why doesn't he come to the door? Why? Help me, help me. This is desperate. Her face burning more than ever before in her life, she hammers on the door. She wants to call out, Let me in, but what if someone hears? Her feet are freezing. Then to the right she hears the lift bell ding and knows she's going to be caught naked and drunk and post-sex in the hallway. It's too much. She dives for the door to the stairwell. It bangs shut behind her just in time. Through the smoked glass she sees a couple weaving down the hall, arm in arm, to their room. Kissing. Then she sees his door open and her boss looking out into the hallway. For some reason she shrinks back against the wall so he doesn't spot her. He looks bleary and tired and intensely irritated. Irritated with her. What a mess. How can she go through with it? How can she go through with the meeting tomorrow, with the drive back to the city, with the next days and weeks and months typing that bloody bastard's boring bloody memos? Never able to tell anyone. Never able to relax. She watches as he closes the door.

Shit, it's cold. Her hands are numb. She scrambles into her clothes, skin crawling with the awful itch of putting her legs back into day-old tights, the awkward hooks of her stupid bra, the ashtray stink of her hair as it falls around her face. The taste in her mouth. Her too-tight skirt and her too-high heels. She's never going to wear anything but jeans ever again. She opens the door, wincing as it squeaks. Pushes the button for the lift, checking over her shoulder that no one's coming.

Thirteen floors down and she's feeling nauseous, her head starting to throb in a sharp and painful way. She staggers out into the reception area, nearly going over on her ankle in these mindless shoes. She makes her way to the desk. They must have a spare key to her room. Presses the buzzer, hears it ringing back in the office behind the desk. Waits. So tired. Suddenly hungry. McDonald's. A big greasy hamburger oozing fat and sauce. Chips caked with salt. A Coke. Where are these people? She holds the buzzer down for a few seconds and leans forward on the desk, rests her head on it, arms hanging slackly by her sides. Feels the pulse in her temple against the marble desktop. Oh for God's sake. She thumps the buzzer again, bashes it with her fist, the tinny ringing of it making her more angry every time. What, are they all asleep? Watching the wrestling on TV? Drunk? Hello? Fuck it, she'll sleep in the car. It can't get any worse than this.

She stumbles around the car park as if it's happening to someone else. One day this might be a funny story to tell someone. Not right now, but it probably has potential. Spice up the sexy details a bit. God, she'd have to make it sound worth it. Where is his goddamn car? What she'd like to do now is take her shoe to the paintwork of every one of these big fat sleek self-satisfied automatic four-wheel drive kiddie-proof stereophonic convertible tinted-window monstrosities. She could so some pretty good damage, scrape them up, put in a couple of dents. She goes to touch one of the cars, feel just what sort of kick it is these guys get out of them, when she gets too close and its alarm goes off, shrill and angry in the darkness. She jumps back as if she's been shouted at. Hits the ground, crawls between two other cars to hide, stockings ripping on the concrete. Shit. Please no one come. Shhh, shhh. The alarm sounds as if it's coming from inside her head. Shut up, shut up. She's too scared to look out over the cars to see if anyone's heard. There must be security guys all over this place. Bangs her head back against the car behind her. Just about brains herself on the door handle. Wait a minute, this is it. His car. Fantastic. She kisses the door. Breathes out at last. Sleep, soon she will be asleep and this will all be over. She controls the shaking in her hand long enough to get the key in the door and open it. Climbs carefully into the passenger seat, locks the door after her. Safe at last. The other car has finally stopped screaming. Maybe she won't be arrested after all. Secretary Screws Boss, Smashes Up Saab. Drunken Doris Dents Daimler. Auto Attack By Tipsy Typist. With the headlines of her evening flashing up in lurid colours behind her eyes, she curls up in the front of her boss's car and falls asleep.

When she wakes up she is cold. She has a crick neck. She is unsure where she is. Oh. That's right. She laughs croakily. It is kind of funny. It's going to be one of those things, she can tell already – flashes of memory will come unbidden to her in the street, at work, in the shower – those cringey moments that make you grit your teeth or suck in your breath or rub your hand across your forehead as if to erase what's there. There are a lot of involuntary blushes stored up from this one. She shakes her head. It's getting light outside. Grey misty light. She looks up at the hotel, sees a couple of lights on. Wonders if he's awake yet. Awake, guilty, going through his stuff for the meeting. Or perhaps he's not guilty. Perhaps he's having a shower, planning to knock on her door and invite her downstairs for breakfast. Yeah, likely story. The fuck wouldn't even let her back in his room. Wanker. No, he'll be trying to pretend he hasn't got a hangover, trying not to think about last night, just get through the meeting and get back to his wife. Thinking, Yes! Probably punching the fucking air. He knows she can't afford repercussions at work. He's got away with it, the tinny bastard. A brief aberration and then everything back to his normal in-control I'm-so-powerful life. She's getting worked up now. The energy feels good. Her head's not that bad either. Could be still drunk. Starving.

Something snaps. That fuck. She's not going to go back up there, pretend nothing's happened, pour fucking coffee for the fucking meeting and take notes. Nuh. He can take his own bloody notes. She's taken enough notes to last a bloody lifetime. Shook enough hands, made enough tea, typed enough minutes. Probably sterile from spending so much time standing by a hot photocopier. Probably got sick building syndrome. Repetitive strain injury. Early Alzheimers, for all she knows. No more. No going back. No way. What she might do instead doesn't seem to matter at this point. She'll think of something. The first thing she's got to do is get something to eat. Get out of this godforsaken shit-heap and get a life. A hamburger as well. She rubs her face. Checks herself out in the rear-vision mirror. Not pretty. Mascara smudges under her eyes, greasy hair, waxy skin. Too bad. No more girly office eyeshadow for her. No more dress code. No more being nice to stupid jerks and stupider cows just because they're more senior than her and make more money.

Money. Damn. It's all back in her room. She's not going to risk going up there. It's not much, she can easily say goodbye to all that old junk. The office clothes she won't be needing any more. The so-called notes she's prepared for the so-called meeting she's supposed to attend, as if she's something more than a glorified secretary. Her reputation. She grins, looking around at the car. Seems like a fair swap. Shoves her hand down the back of the seat till she finds enough coins for breakfast. It's true, she thinks, remembering a conversation from last night, she really hasn't done enough travelling. What a good time to start. She slides over into the driver's seat. Can she handle one of these big cars? A breeze. The key slots into the ignition with a satisfying click. Pulling out of the car park on to the main road, she runs over her options.

# *rosie and some other people*

This is a story about Rosie and Mark. About Rosie and Mark
and Lynn. Or about Lynn, and Rosie and Mark (if you
happen to be Lynn). Adam, a minor player, would probably
call it *Adam's Tragedy*. Anya wouldn't want to know. And
Mark – Mark might try for an appropriate song title.
Something along the lines of 'You Can't Always Get What
You Want', perhaps. But then that might be granting Mark
a sense of humour about himself that he doesn't really have.
Anyway, seeing that the song would be about Rosie (sort
of), it seems fair to say that the story is about Rosie. Rosie
and some other people.

It mostly happened because Rosie decided to take a night
class. Lynn was roped in to help her decide on the best one.
They spent a whole afternoon going down the list of
available classes and discussing what sort of man would be
likely to take which. Rosie's first choice was pottery, imagining someone clever with his hands and remembering the
scene from *Ghost*. But when she rang to enrol, the woman
on the phone was terribly sorry, pottery was already over-

subscribed this term and the next. Ceramic painting still had some places unfilled, however . . . Rosie mouthed Ceramic painting? to Lynn, who mouthed What? Rosie tried to mime painting a plate but she dropped the receiver and, feeling how cross the woman must be getting with her, grabbed it and said, Yes, yes, ceramic painting would be great. She gave her details and went downtown with Lynn straight away to mail the cheque. So, given everything that happened, although she knew it was crazy, she couldn't help but feel a little bit responsible.

She turned out to be fairly bad at ceramic painting. The first week, the teacher had them all paint a bird on a saucer. Rosie had visions of Italian bowls with naively rendered ducks and farmyard scenes. She thought this style would be easy, but when she found that she couldn't control the thickness of lines she was painting and that her hands shook, she was disappointed. She looked at her wobbly half-chicken and couldn't understand it. The guy next to her smiled and gestured to his saucer, which had a couple of seagull 'm's on it.

—I can't draw, he said. —So I do these.

Rosie smiled back.

Yes, she said to Lynn at home later, there was a guy there. And she'd talked to him! He was OK looking, too. Not Rosie's type though, more Lynn's. They often agreed it was just as well they were attracted to different types of men. Rosie didn't admit it though, hardly even to herself, but she had kind of a crush on Lynn's boyfriend Adam. This was one reason why she thought the night classes might be a good idea.

Mark, as the seagull man was called, seemed to be a nice guy. A nice guy with a girlfriend, Rosie found out when they went for coffee after class. Because he was more a Lynn-type than a Rosie-type she decided she didn't mind too much. Mark was a musician and doing the night classes because he didn't want to limit his range of creative expression. Rosie understood. She tried to come up with a reason for doing the course that would sound just as impressive, but he didn't ask her so it was all right. They talked about music and he told her about his band, Kidney. Things were going great for them, they were this close to a record deal. They hadn't played a gig in a while but they practised all the time, they were all totally into it. Great guys, too. Well, the lead singer was a bit of an asshole, but, you know, lead singers. Rosie thought she knew, but she wasn't positive. She wondered if having briefly gone out with one counted. He asked her what she did and she explained how she'd been unemployed since graduating from a hair-dressing course four months ago. He told her he liked her haircut. She said thanks. She explained that she didn't cut her own hair. He said he also liked her nose-ring. He'd been thinking of getting one himself. She told him it didn't hurt too much but if you were unlucky it could go septic. They swapped phone numbers.

Over the next eight weeks, Rosie's confidence with ceramics grew. Soon she was bringing home plates with abstract patterns (easier to hide the mistakes) that she

displayed on a shelf in the kitchen. She wondered about
getting a stall at the market, but Lynn said best not to rush
things. Mark was working on a seagull series that he planned
to give his girlfriend for her birthday. He and Rosie went for
coffee or a drink after most classes. He introduced Rosie to
his girlfriend, Anya. Rosie quite liked Anya but was intimi-
dated by her.

—She's one of those dark, intense women, she told Lynn.
—I feel stupid when she's in the room.

—Oh, one of those, said Lynn, —Like, a man's woman.

—No, like a woman's woman, said Rosie, —That's why
she's scary.

—So, bond with her. Talk about how fucked men are, or
something.

—Yeah, right, said Rosie, —or something.

Rosie was clearing up when she found a shopping list in
Lynn's handwriting. It said

> veges
> pasta
> razors
> a gun
> teabags
> olive oil
> a new life

Rosie put the piece of paper back where she found it. She
checked the next day but it was gone. Lynn came home
from Adam's and they sat in the kitchen, drinking tea, not
talking.

The week after the course finished, Mark rang Rosie to see if she could meet him after practice. He said he had a surprise for her. Practice must have gone late, because Rosie sat in a bar alone for almost half an hour, fielding looks from boys and wondering why no one offered to buy her a drink. When she finally saw Mark pushing his way through the crowd she turned her back so he could surprise her. He said boo in her ear and she spun round to see his face, grinning, adorned with a nose stud and two eyebrow rings.

—I did it! he said. —How do you like it? I don't look gay or anything?

—No, you look great, said Rosie. —Cool.

They sat opposite each other in a booth. It was hot. Rosie's arm itched and she scratched it. Soon she was scratching it almost uncontrollably. She didn't want Mark to think she had fleas, but the scratching felt too good to stop. She would have liked to have a go at her head as well, but that seemed really gross. After a while Mark said, —You don't do that, do you?

—What do you mean?

—That scratching thing. Anya used to do it so bad she's got scars all up her arm. She'd draw blood, man.

—Oh, like self-mutilation, said Rosie. —No, I don't do that. She felt bad because in a way she wished she could do that, and be fucked-up and glamorous.

—That's what I like about you, guy, said Mark.

Rosie didn't ask him to elaborate.

–

—I like having a male friend, Rosie said to Lynn. —You
know, just like a friend friend?

—Great, said Lynn, —I'm more into guys for the dick
thing myself.

—Thanks, babe, said Adam on his way from the bedroom
to the bathroom.

—If only it were that simple, said Lynn. —Toast?


Rosie continued to look for work, but the picture was pretty
bleak. Anya was a make-up assistant on films and things, and
Rosie had thought she might be able to ask around for her.
But Anya didn't offer, and Rosie felt funny about bringing it
up herself. She was even more uncomfortable around Anya
now, and curious to see what was hiding under the long
tight sleeves she always wore. Money was becoming a bit of
a problem. Her parents said she was welcome to stay with
them for a while, but she couldn't think of anything worse.
Maybe if they were divorced. But, live with the two of them
together under one roof – she'd rather get a job at a hair
salon in the suburbs.


She bumped into Mark and Anya in town.

—Come for a drink, said Mark.

Anya said nothing.

—I don't know, I've got to be, I'm supposed to . . . Rosie
felt utterly lame. Mark put his head on the side and raised
his eyebrows in a puppy dog impersonation.

—Go on, just a quick one.

Anya sort of smiled. Rosie decided to say yes just to stop Mark making that stupid face.

The music was a bit loud for conversation but Rosie didn't feel comfortable not talking.

—How's work going? she shouted.

—Oh, you know, said Anya.

There was a pause.

—Yeah, shouted Rosie.

—Excuse me. Anya went over to a table of women who were drinking margaritas and laughing raucously. Rosie watched them greet her with hugs and kisses. She felt as if she'd been cast in a role she didn't audition for.

—She hasn't had a job in two weeks, said Mark. —That blasé act's just a wank.

—Oh, said Rosie. She understood she'd somehow been let off the hook, but she wasn't sure about hearing Mark slag off his girlfriend.

Later, when Anya had come back to their table and they'd each had several drinks, Rosie stood up to leave.

—Oh, you can't go, said Anya.

Rosie looked at her. Anya hadn't given one indication before now that she was enjoying her company. She sat down again. She remembered a video she'd seen with Elizabeth Taylor in it. Something about tormenting guests. Mark went to get another round.

—Look at him, said Anya. —The dude. You know why he did that crazy night school thing?

Rosie shook her head.

—He read somewhere that Eddie Vedder does ceramic

painting. Anya laughed. —Can you believe it? In his dreams!

Rosie laughed too, despite herself.

—Musicians are such cowboys, said Anya. —It's the same in film. Christ, I'm surrounded by them. Have you got a boyfriend?

—No, said Rosie. —Not at the moment.

Mark came back with drinks. —What's up, guys?

—Nothing, they both said.

—Do you think Anya's jealous of your friendship with Mark? Lynn asked.

—No, said Rosie, —Why would she be?

—Come on, said Lynn, —Do you think she is?

—Maybe, said Rosie. —I don't know, maybe.

Which is why Rosie didn't go to see Kidney play the first gig they'd had since she met Mark. She didn't think he would notice that she wasn't there, but when she rang him the next day he sounded very distant.

—They dug it, was all he would say about the gig.

—Sorry I couldn't make it.

—Whatever. I gotta go practise. We're playing again next week. If you're interested.

Rosie asked Lynn if she wanted to go.

—What are they called? Kidney? I'd rather lose one.

—Don't say that, said Rosie. —What if it comes true?

—I don't think Mark and his friends have got that much karmic pull, honey. But you have a good time.

—

Rosie looked around the bar for Anya but couldn't see her.
There were some other people she knew so she went over
and stood with them. The band played for about an hour. It
was very loud. Mark played the guitar. Rosie wasn't sure if
it was the bass guitar or the other sort. He stood quite still
and looked quite serious while the lead singer twitched
around, threw his hair forward over his shoulders, and held
his microphone almost in his mouth. He crouched down a
lot, like Bono, and sometimes would go from a whisper to a
scream so fast that Rosie felt jumpy. She thought Mark was
good, except occasionally he seemed to be playing in a
different rhythm from everyone else. Some people danced
and some just stood around nodding. Mark waved from the
band's table during their break, but it wasn't till the set was
finished that he came over.

—What do you think?

—It was great, said Rosie. —I dug it.

—Cool, cool, said Mark. —It wasn't like, our best gig
ever. What did you think of that song, 'Chain Me To The
Rock'?

—Which one was that again? asked Rosie.

—You know, it goes, 'Chain me to the rock, chain me
to the rock, eat out my liver, chain me to the rock,' Mark
sang.

—Oh yeah. It was great.

—Yeah? I wrote that one.

—Really? It was really great.

—Yeah, I want the band to play more of my songs, but
you know, Jeff's an asshole. Mark snorted. —Lead singers.

—Yeah, right, said Rosie. —Hey, where's Anya?

—Oh, she didn't come, said Mark, —we broke up.

—Oh, Mark, said Rosie. —Oh. I'm sorry.

—Yeah, I don't really want to talk about it. Hey, let's get out of here.

They went to another bar and Mark talked about it. Anya had got together with some cameraman. Rosie felt terrible for Mark. She'd been broken up with a few times herself and she knew how horrible it was. Mark said, yeah, well, that was her trip, life goes on, you know, he wasn't going to waste time crying about it, things were going great for Kidney, they were this close to a record deal so, you know, hey, it's Anya's loss, right, guy?

—Absolutely, said Rosie, except she was a bit drunk by now and had to say the word two or three times before it came out right.

Lynn came into Rosie's room and pulled open the curtains.

—It stinks in here, she said. —Are you too hung to talk?

—Mm, said Rosie, trying to unglue her eyes.

—OK, then listen, said Lynn. —I think I'm going off Adam. I can't stand for him to touch me anymore. Looking at him gives me the creeps. I have to wear clothes to bed.

—You go to bed fully dressed? Rosie wondered if she needed to throw up.

—You know, in a T-shirt. And knickers. I can't stand to get naked with him. What am I going to do?

—What about the dick thing?

—I don't know. I don't know how it happened. One minute I was right into it, the next minute I want to gag if he comes near me. I have no idea.

Rosie sat up in bed. Her brain felt like it had swelled up in the night and was too big for her skull. She lay back down again.

—What am I going to do?

—Why don't you talk to him.

—Talk to him? said Lynn. —Saying what? Hey, Adam, you know how we've had great sex for six months, well, now you make me sick. Good one.

—You know, say you need time out, said Rosie. Her stomach was feeling dangerous and she found it was easier to keep her eyes closed. She wanted some time out herself, right now, for as long as it took to get over this thing.

—Maybe, said Lynn. —I feel so bad about it, like I've—

The phone rang. Lynn ran for it.

—I'm not here, Rosie called after her, in as loud a voice as she could manage.

Later, she realized it was a bad idea and she probably only thought of it because of the alcohol still in her bloodstream, but at the time it seemed quite sensible to get Mark and Lynn together and see if they were interested.

Mark showed up on one of his post-practice highs. He sat in their kitchen drumming everything in sight – the table, his knees, Rosie's arm – slightly out of time with the record that was playing. Lynn seemed kind of uptight. She did all the

dishes and tidied up around them while Mark talked about
the band. Rosie asked what he was going to do now with his
seagull plate collection.

—Oh, nothing, he said, reaching for a cigarette. —It's broken.

—What happened? asked Rosie, unsure if this was safe
ground to get on to with Lynn in the room.

—I broke it, said Mark. —You know, I made it for her,
and she—. Well, she still wants it, but she just, she can just
get fucked, right?

—So, what? You smashed it? asked Rosie.

—Yeah.

—In front of her?

—Yeah.

—What did she do?

—Nothing much. She just kind of left, you know.

—Wow, Mark, that's really intense, said Rosie. Over
Mark's head she could see Lynn rolling her eyes. She
suddenly felt hot and sick again.

—Ceramics are pretty stupid anyway, said Mark. —Hey,
I've gotta go.

Rosie saw him out and went into her room and quietly
shut the door. She sat on her bed. She picked up a pillow
and held it to her stomach. Lynn changed a record in the
next room. Rosie tried to cry. She couldn't.


Lynn walked around the house, singing.

> I squander all my food
> I never ever sleep in the nude

—What's that? said Rosie.

—Uh? That Liz Phair song – the pitbull in the basement one.

—But those aren't the words are they? said Rosie, wanting to just shut up, wishing she didn't have to make sure everything was right all the time.

Lynn didn't stop singing. Rosie felt rebuked, and relieved.

She arranged to meet Mark at the Social Welfare. They sat next to each other on a couch. Mark ignored the No Smoking sign.

—Have you spoken to Anya? Rosie asked.

—Who? Man, I don't care if I never see her again. Bitch.

Rosie laughed her nervous laugh. —At least you haven't got, like, her name tattooed all over your body or something.

There was a silence. Mark stared straight ahead.

—Mark? You haven't.

—Nah, don't be stupid.

Someone called Mark's name. He followed the man to an interview booth around the corner.

—Oh my God, Rosie said to herself. —Oh, that's scary.

—You know, Rosie said to Lynn, —Mark calls me 'guy' all the time. Like, What's happening, guy, or Chill, guy – I hate it.

—Well, you're the one going on about how great it is to have this platonic friendship, said Lynn.

—Yeah, but do I have to become a guy to have that?

—So, tell him you don't like it.

—Yeah. Um, he's coming over tonight.

—This set's going to be so great. Mark flicked his hair off his face and counted on his fingers, —We're doing 'Chain Me To The Rock' first, which is excellent because it's such an excellent opening song, then 'If It Has A Face Eat It', then 'Spear', then a cover of . . . uh—

—'My Dick Is So Huge It's Going To Eclipse The Sun'? suggested Lynn. Rosie kicked her.

—Yeah, good one, guy, said Mark. —Nah, it's that Hendrix one, you know.

—Oh yeah, of course, said Lynn, —I know. Well, excuse me, Mark, I'm going to have to go and shave my pubic hair.

—Did you have to be like that? asked Rosie later.

—Like what? said Lynn. —Like, did he even notice?

—Well, he didn't say anything.

—There you go then. My point exactly.

—But I'm sure he noticed, Rosie said.

Mark gave Rosie a present. It was a bar of soap with a picture of a sailing ship on it.

—I had one of these when I was a kid, said Rosie, not sure if she should hug him or not. —The picture lasts as long as the soap does, right?

—Yeah, said Mark, tucking a strand of Rosie's hair behind her ear for her, —as long as the soap.

They looked at each other. Rosie sniffed the soap.

—It's plastic or something, said Mark. —The picture I mean.

They were drunk.

—How old were you? Lynn asked Mark.

—Uh, fifteen. Yeah.

—Was she your girlfriend? Lynn put a sarcastic spin on the word.

—Nah, just a girl from school—

—What was her name? Lynn reached across to Mark for the ashtray. —And don't say you can't remember.

—Her name was Mandy. Amanda something. I wanted her to be my girlfriend, man. But she was going out with my best mate. Mark laughed. —Pretty bad, huh?

—Not really, said Lynn. —I've heard worse.

Rosie stood up to get a drink of water. She realized how unsteady she was. Her face felt slack. She ran the water and held her wrists under it. Lynn and Mark were still talking.

—I held out till I was about eighteen, said Lynn. —My parents put the fear of God about it in me.

—Why? Mark moved into Rosie's empty seat, next to Lynn.

—They're Jehovah's Witness.

—No shit.

Rosie stood at the sink and wondered if it was worth calling Lynn on this lie.

—Yeah. They're fuck-ups. I still can't do it without getting drunk.

—Really? Mark was trying to light the wrong end of a

cigarette. Rosie felt a sudden urge to knock their heads together.

—Yeah, said Lynn, smiling her best smile, —but when I get there I'm great.

Mark dropped his cigarette on the floor. —I gotta have a slash.

He left for the bathroom. Rosie wanted more than anything to be lying down in her quiet bed. She moved past Lynn to the door. Lynn grabbed her arm.

—Look, she said, and her face was very close to Rosie's and a bit distorted, —what do you want? Are you deciding that you want Mark now?

—No, said Rosie, pulling her arm out of Lynn's grip. —No, I don't want him. You have him. Fuck like snakes. Do what you like.

She bumped into Mark on her way out the door.

—Rabbits, she said to him. —I meant rabbits.

Mark smiled at her, went into the kitchen and closed the door behind him.

Rosie lay in her bed. She said the alphabet backwards to stop the memories she was having of her own first time. The room spun around her.

Lynn was holding a *Magic Eye* book up to her nose when Rosie came into her room.

—I nicked it from a bookshop, she said. —I'm glad I didn't pay money for it. I can't see any of the pictures.

Rosie sat next to her on the bed. —What's that supposed to be?

—Love-hearts I think. Maybe you need to be stoned.
They squinted at the page.
—It's stupid, isn't it? said Rosie.
—Yeah. Hey, Rose, I'm sorry about, you know.
—That's OK, said Rosie. —Adam rang.
—Oh, said Lynn.
—Hey, I can see them, said Rosie. —I think.


They spent the day cleaning the house. They were about to go for a walk. Lynn of course got to the phone first.
—Hello?
Rosie didn't know why she made such a performance out of diving for it. She herself was quite happy to let it ring, these days.
—Oh, hi, Mark. How are you?
Rosie flicked to the TV page in the paper.
—No it's Lynn. Yeah, hang on.
Lynn put the receiver down on the table. —It's for you, she said. She left the room.
Rosie picked up the phone. It was heavy. She could hear Lynn running a bath.
—Hello? Her voice came out in a whisper. She heard a click. Then music. A guitar, some drums, and Mark's voice, soft and slightly out of tune.

> The sun is bright tonight
> Give me some of that orange
> Come into the garden, Rosie
> Come and see the midnight sun

*rosie and some other people*

> The air is light tonight
> Nothing rhymes with orange
> Got to tell you, listen, Rosie
> I don't know if you're the one
>
> But it feels like it
> Rosie, my Rose
> Rosie, my Rose
> Rosie, Rose Rose
> My my my Rose

The tape deck clicked off. Rosie rubbed her hand over her eyes.

—Are you there? said Mark.

—Yeah, said Rosie, —I'm here. Look, Mark—, she felt all wringy and sick inside. She clutched the arm of her chair. Some of the material ripped under her fingers.

—Yeah? said Mark. —Do you like it?

—Look, Mark, she said again. She made a sour-taste face. Her shoulders were up around her ears.

—Mark, it doesn't work like that.

There. She'd said it. She breathed out. She waited to hear Mark hang up. But he didn't.

—Why not? he said.

# local girl goes missing

My mother was an amateur photographer. Dad gave her a camera for a wedding present. It out-lasted the marriage. None of us girls were allowed to touch it. It was so old-fashioned, second-hand when he bought it, that we all chipped in and got her a new one for her fortieth birthday. She said thank you and kissed us but she kept on using the old one. Most of the photographs in this album are taken by her.

Here's Bernadette at Piha. Sand all round her mouth, she must have been eating it. I don't know what she's pointing at – maybe something one of us fished out of a rock pool. That's Lion Rock in the background. Bern first climbed it when she was about two or something. I never did of course. But Bern and Therese loved it, they were always on at Mum to take them up there. I'd stay on the beach watching the patterns my black shadow made on the black sand. Iron sand that got so hot under your feet you couldn't keep still. If you ran down the dunes wearing jandals they'd flick the sand up onto the back of your calves, stinging like someone was throwing lit matches at you. Black sand, blowholes and huge, huge waves. That's what a beach was to me, burning hot feet and caves with water crashing through them and waves as high as the sky. I have a recurring dream, standing ankle-deep in water watching a wave rise up before me getting bigger and bigger until it's all I can see, and I can't run away and I know it's going to swamp me. Well, I know it's symbolic and I don't need an analyst to tell me what it means, but it always makes me think of Piha. When we'd stay out there for a week and Mum'd take her watch off and there was no such thing as lunch-time, you just ate when you got hungry. A-frame holiday houses and vans with long-haired men and women who'd come out to cook damper or run around naked in the surf. Every year someone would drown from swimming in jeans. You had to watch out for rips, if a rip gets you you don't fight it because that'll only tire you out. You swim sideways with it, along the beach until you get through it and you can swim back to shore. Sometimes you can get caught in a rip even if you're not very far out. Or you can get dumped. I got dumped a lot when I was too small for the waves and it slams down on you and your face scrapes the sand at the bottom and you kick, trying to find which way the surface of the water is – that's if you're unlucky and it turns you upside-down, or if you're easily disoriented, like me. Sometimes huge blue-bottles would be washed up, and we'd poke them with sticks. It always surprised me how rubbery and resistant they were. My stick would never pierce them, it would just bounce back in my hand. Later, when Therese was older and boys hung around, they'd pick the jellyfish up and throw them at each other. My biggest fear was that someone would throw a blue-bottle at me and that I'd cry. Maybe they could tell that, and that's why nobody ever did it. Therese would have punched them if they had.

We'd all get sunburnt, and Mum would have criss-crosses on the backs of her legs from lying in the hammock, and the sand would never quite wash off our feet before we came inside so the floor was always covered in grit. A friend of Mum's would come and stay for the last weekend, bringing her kids, and we'd go out in the dark after dinner and have bravery competitions. Sometimes I'd sneak away from these and go back to the house early, reading on my bunk or in a corner of the open-plan room while Mum and her friend drank wine and talked. Once I came into the house and saw Mum crying while her friend sat with her arm around her. It was the first time I ever saw my mother cry. They hadn't noticed I was standing there so I went back outside and walked along the dunes, digging my toes through the cold night sand, till I found the others playing Logan's Run by the pine trees.

Anyway. That's Piha. And that's Bern. Look at her. She was the happiest child you can imagine.

John'll think I'm weird if he comes in and sees me holding this photo album, breathing in its musty smell, not painting the kitchen skirting-boards or sanding the table or whatever DIY task I'm supposed to be doing. It's just about falling apart, this book. The spine's broken. I used to be scared of tearing the sheets of tissue that cover the photographs.

When everyone was out of the house I'd get this from Mum's cupboard and look at the photos for hours. Half my memories, I don't know if they're from what actually happened or from looking in this album. When I remember my childhood up to the age of about ten, it's mostly in black and white. But the sun was always shining. That's what everybody says, isn't it? We all had bare feet and the sun shone night and day.

This is a good one, the three of us in our confirmation dresses. I don't think Mum ever believed in God – she was brought up Presbyterian or something, and stopped going to church when she left home. But she always had this obsession with Catholicism. So theatrical, she'd say, lighting a stick of incense, so corrupt – can't you smell it? And she'd shiver, smiling, the way she did when she told us about Molly Whuppy and the Bridge of the Single Hair. She never knew much about it, Catholicism, or what the rituals were supposed to mean, but she'd talk about Popes and gold, and cook us fish on Friday, and whenever a friend of hers was having a crisis – which seemed to be often – she'd light a candle for them. My mother's friends were always leaving their husbands or being left or getting pregnant or going into communes or losing their jobs. And in the marital crisis stakes, I guess Mum was no exception. This photo's from when Therese was thirteen and Mum made us all long white frocks. I was eleven, and Bern was far too young, she was eight or something, but Mum wanted us all to dress up together. None of us had any idea what confirmation was supposed to be so we just put on our white dresses and

Mum gave us each a glass of red wine. The worst part was, Dad rang up and Bern answered the phone and said, Sorry, Dad, I can't talk now I have to go and finish my wine. He rang back furious but Mum pulled the phone out of the wall and put Janis Joplin on and we all danced to 'Me & Bobby McGee' till I threw up from spinning around too much. That's why we've all got Catholic names, Mum named us from the Oxford Dictionary of Saints. Dad hated it, but he couldn't stop her – the deal was, she'd picked the girls' names and he could name the boys. He'd had enough of her after three girls and went off to have boys with Angela.

John's painting the outside of the house. We haven't been here very long and it needs a lot of work. John likes that. Something to do on the weekends. He likes the physical side of it. He's more comfortable not thinking. I don't know where he's gone. I went to take him a cup of tea just before but he's disappeared. His brushes are still there, and his stepladder. It looks strrange, as if he'd stepped off the ladder and vanished into the air. Last month I was in town and I saw a pushchair lying on its side on a street corner, empty. I came home and told John about it but he didn't think it was unusual. I shouldn't have said that, about him not thinking. It's not a nice thing to say.

Mum converted the garden shed into a dark-room. I used to love it but fear it, the chemical smell and the orange light. She made us pinhole cameras once, which seemed silly to me, like the phones we'd make out of paper cups and bits of string. Cardboard and sticky tape – it wasn't as exciting as the real thing. The girls at school had their own automatic cameras, or even Polaroids. They were the best. I remember watching Mum developing photographs, moving her hand over the print while it lay in the fluid to show me how she could make the shadows blur. Watching the picture come out of the paper like magic. Sunday mornings when Therese slept in and Bern was listening to the requests on the radio, I'd go down and watch Mum making photographs. Bern didn't know, but Mum used to tell the radio stories too, and she did them better. And she ran and he ran, and he ran and she ran, until they came to the Bridge of the Single Hair. Or Little Toot, or Red Riding Hood. Mum could make her voice go so low when she told those stories I had to hug myself, frightened. I knew it was only her but sometimes in the light she looked like a different person, orange and shadowy, her hands moving like someone else's hands, picking up the corners of the paper with tongs and pegging them to dry. For all the pictures she took of us, I didn't ever get used to seeing my own face come out of the paper at me, dark and light and never how I imagined I must really look.

This is the one that was in the paper. Therese ran away, the year after we were confirmed, the year she slammed her door every morning and called Mum Mother, the year she started going out late and smoking cigarettes in the house. Mum threatened to send her to live with Dad but it was useless, Therese knew Mum would rather die first. Thinking about it now, I wonder whether Dad would have taken her, anyway. His and Angela's twins were young and we didn't hardly see him in those days. It's funny what you get used to. Sometimes I missed him being there and twirling us around or grabbing our ankles when we ran past, or I missed just watching him and Therese playing cards after dinner. But Bern, you wouldn't think she remembered him at all. She never once asked where he was or when he was coming back, she just kept on like he'd never even lived in the same house. Therese missed him though, more than me, she missed him but she hated him at the same time. And when she ran away I was sure she'd gone to his place, but Mum eventually rang and checked – she didn't want to, I could tell – and Therese wasn't there. This was on the second day, and that was the second time I saw my mother cry. She cried at the kitchen table and then she made me and Bern come and sit with her and pray to Saint Francis. According to my mother he was the patron saint of lost things and even though Therese wasn't a thing, like your house keys or your earrings or something, we still prayed for her to be found. I didn't know how to pray, what you were supposed to do, so I just shut my eyes and said please, please, please. Then Mum rang the police, and then she made us tidy our room before they came round. There was a man and a lady and they talked quietly to my mother and she talked loudly to them. She showed them the photograph she'd taken of Therese for her fourteenth birthday and they took it to put in the paper. It was there the next day, in the back, with a headline saying Local Girl Goes Missing. Therese had so much make-up on in the picture she looked about nineteen, not fourteen. Mum said it would probably start perverts hunting her down instead of help anyone find her. Therese was away for three more days and Mum got thinner and whiter and angrier with every one of them. She borrowed her friend Jennifer's car and drove around and around at night, looking, not coming home until it was light. It was the longest I knew her not to go into her dark-room. I started going in there on my own then, sitting on the floor in the murky light, singing to myself. I was in there when I heard the car pull up and Mum and Therese get out, shouting at each other. I got out and looked in the kitchen window and saw Therese standing in the middle of the room, a wreck, crying, and Mum putting dinner on, banging the plates down so hard I could hear it from the shed, but she was smiling. And then Therese said something and Mum's face went soft and she turned around and Therese slumped into her arms and cried and cried.

Mum never got the original photo back from the paper so she cut out the clipping and stuck it here in this album. The only one of her photographs ever to be in print she said later, when she was laughing and joking again. Therese does look beautiful in this picture. She was self-conscious about the gap between her teeth so she'd never smile. In most of these photos Bern and I are grinning away like idiots while Therese looks guarded and intense.

Our school photos are in here too, all of them. Row after row of children, girls in the front, boys in the back, dressed in their best clothes, chorusing cheese, or underwear, or whatever word the photographer picked to get us looking at the camera and alert. School photo days were always a fight for whatever was our favourite bit of clothing at the time.

Mum had signed a petition to abolish the school uniform, but on photo day she'd stand in the middle of the kitchen while the three of us kicked and punched and hissed our way around the house, her eyes to the ceiling, saying Why did I sign that stupid bit of paper? And usually the desired object – a lace top of Therese's one year, my jean jacket the next – would be confiscated and hidden and we'd all have to wear something like our most hated brown cardigans. In some of these photos you can't tell Therese and Bern apart. You have to look at the year and class number on the board, always held by the prettiest girl in the middle of the front row, to figure it out. And in some of my class photos, you can't find me at all. You scan the rows until you think you've seen everyone, and I'm still not there. When you do find me, second row back, fourth from the left, you wonder why my face looks so blank when everyone else's looks normal. Not just expressionless blank, but literally blank, almost whited out, featureless, a smudge. It's probably just a combination of my paleness and the flash bulb. Or something.

Look, there's even a photo of me and John, just after we got together. We met during my half-hearted attempt to be part of the social scene at university. I was standing by the door at a party, thinking about leaving, and he came up and asked me if I wanted to dance. I told him I couldn't dance, and he said there was no way I could be a worse dancer than him, and so I said all right. He was right, he was a terrible dancer, so we stopped and talked, or tried to with the music so loud. I was a very earnest student. But John didn't seem to mind, and when someone fell on the stereo and the party started breaking up, he offered to walk me home. I guess it was because he left me at the door and didn't try to grope me that I decided that I wanted him.

And after another party the next weekend I sought him out and took him home and opened for the first time the packet of condoms my mother had given me when I started university. This is one thing the Catholics are dead wrong about, honey, she said, while I stared at the packet, horrified, mortified that she would do such a thing. It almost put me off going to bed with John, knowing that she'd provided the condoms, but I decided that as long as it was only him I went to bed with, she wasn't getting her way entirely. At least it meant I could stop going to parties. And things just went on from there really, it was somehow easier to be with him than not be with him.

There are pictures tucked into the back cover that I've never seen before. This is strange, things not being how they were, as if some established order has been shuffled around and shifted. I'm not sure that I like it. Perhaps she got sick of arranging things properly. Maybe she took them out and couldn't be bothered putting them back right. I asked her not so long ago if she ever looked in here any more. She said, No, dahlink – that old thing? Never. But she must have had them out recently – these are early ones. Mum cooking over a gas burner on a camping holiday; Dad asleep with the paper over his face; the view of a lake; Mum outside a huge Catholic cathedral surrounded by pigeons. Photographs of them before we ever existed. Black polo-necks and stove-pipe trousers, Beatles haircuts and sunglasses, huge smiles on both of their faces. They must be younger in these than I am now. They look it. They look young and clean and beautiful. Then come baby pictures, and sandpits, and paddling pools. The five of us, taken by a fellow tramper on a hill – my eyes shut, Bern like a little fat-legged doll, Therese looking off in the distance already. One more of Mum and Dad with their arms around each other. Now some just of us four, or a tree, or Mum's friends dressed up to go out. Our lives together, our lives apart.

This album drives John crazy, I suppose. He only found out about it last week when we cleared out Mum's house. He sat down, Therese and Bernadette on either side of him at that old kitchen table, and turned each page as if it was made of gold. Therese and Bern laughed and cried and sighed over the pictures, pointing things out, remembering. I wrapped cups and plates into newspaper, my back to them, and I could feel John's eyes staring at me, then the pictures, at me, then the pictures. We all had a bit to drink and my sisters started on stories, one after the other, about as many untrue as there were true. Every now and then one of them would go to the album for proof, finding the right picture with triumph. See, you did dye your hair that stupid colour – look, there was a hole in the bottom of that tree, I can see the Easter egg wrapper hidden in it – there, they did hug each other sometimes. Well, maybe it was for the camera. God, that dress, how could she wear that? But, look there – you look beautiful. No, I hate that one, awful. Oh, there's Cath, said Bern, eyes closed as usual. Mum only had to bring her camera out and you'd start that nervous blink.

Later, in the car on the way home, John's silence got bigger and bigger until he said, Why don't you ever tell me stories? Why do I have to hear everything about you from your sisters? Everything looks normal in those pictures, it's not like you had a worse childhood than anyone else. I didn't say anything. I looked out the window at the suburb that I grew up in. You're pathologically secretive, Catherine, he said. I can't stand it. I thought about Mum's house empty with all the lights out and the cutlery in boxes and I didn't say anything. Then today in the mail was the album. The note from Therese said they wanted me to have it because they knew I'd take care of it best. This is the kind of decision Therese and Bernadette make about me all the time.

This really is the most hideous photograph. My mother set the camera on automatic and ran back to put her arms around her last boyfriend, and laughed, and as the shutter clicked they were both laughing, lips pulled up over their gums, Mum's mouth open so wide you can almost see her tonsils, her last boyfriend short and pink and shiny, caught up in her long thin arms. He's so short, isn't he, Cath, she said to me when I first met him. I'd gone to visit and we were introduced, then he went into the kitchen to make us drinks. She pulled a face as soon as he was out of sight, and laughed. God isn't he short, she said, he's practically a dwarf. I laughed too, I couldn't help it. The way she said it – duh-warf – I was in love with the way she said that word. We kept laughing, and the last boyfriend, the duh-warf, came out of the kitchen to see what was so funny. Nothing, my mother said, and as soon as he was gone again she

whispered, Rumpelstiltskin! and shrieked with laughter.
Suddenly I was back in her dark room with the Sunday
morning fairy stories and I had to bite my top lip hard in
case I cried. He didn't last long, the last boyfriend, but he
kept my mother laughing. Oh, she said, you're so lucky
John's not a duh-warf, Cathy – good for the genes, I don't
have to worry about that any more you see. No, Mum, he's
not a dwarf, I said. And he's not. He's a giant.

Last night in bed, John asked did I think it was a good
time to have a baby. He didn't say what he meant by now
being a good time, but I knew. I said, but *I'm* still a baby.
He laughed. I guess he thought I was joking.

I'd thought there'd be a picture here from the day Mum
and I went to the beach last month. I remember now she
wouldn't let me take any.

—No cameras, dahlink. Her attempt to make the sunglasses seem a glamorous accessory of choice, not a necessity.
So we just walked, scraping sticks along the sand, picking up
shells, studying them. Not far, because she got tired. Then
we stood for a bit and watched the waves come down on
top of one another. On the way back to the car, she stopped
and poked at a clump of thick black kelp lying by the water's
edge.

—Like the unconscious, isn't it, she said, lifting a strand
of its sleek rubber with her stick and letting it fall.

I laughed. —That's such a you thing to say, Mum.

She grinned – I hadn't seen her look so pleased for a
while. —Do you really think so?

Why didn't I take a photograph then? Now I'm not sure

if I can even remember the day right. And there's nobody else to ask.

Another thing my mother said to me, that day on the beach. Oh. It seems so much longer than a month ago. She told me she was seeing things. I've taken to seeing things, Cath, she said, in the voice that was older than she was, the voice she used for effect, or maybe just for her own sense of theatre. I thought she meant visions, you know, the Catholic thing getting out of control. Don't be silly, she said, I'm not seeing the Virgin Mary coming for me on a surf board or anything, sweetheart, nothing that exciting. She laughed and wheezed. I waited for her to stop, in the way I'd got used to waiting, patiently, just watching her with a calm expression on my face until she was all right again. She explained that the things she was seeing were peripheral, in the corners, quick flashes of movement or shape, an alien scuttling out of sight or a figure bending over. She would turn to follow these with her gaze, but there was never anything there. Are you worried about it, Mum? I said. She said, no, not really, it was most likely just side-effects. She didn't mind her world suddenly being populated with half-explained shapes, these visitors to the edge of frame who made their presence briefly known and then were gone. It's funny now, looking through this album I expect to see one of them, captured on the side of a photograph, the way they can sometimes take a photo and capture a ghost. But in all these pictures there's nothing there. I don't think that really matters though. I don't think that makes them any less real.

And I guess, then, that it's my own fault I've stuck myself

in this boring home. My own fault I try to read signs into empty pushchairs and black and white photographs. My own fault that I can't tell John that what I really want to do is travel, and without him, and that I don't care if the bathroom is painted avocado or white and the last thing I want to do is have children with him or with anyone, that I've just buried my mother and she's still more alive than I have ever felt.

In this one she took of John and me together, in the first year, I think maybe I can see some bravery in my face. It might only be because I'm standing next to John and he looks like such a rock, such a part of something solid, that I look like the kind of person who could untie myself from that. Who could untie myself from the earth and gasp as the ropes fall away and as I start lifting up into the air, gasp with the shock of it, but with the pleasure of it as well.

# *you can hear the boats go by*

The vegetables look unnaturally healthy. They are shiny and wet and arranged in piles according to colour. The season is changing. Fancy lettuce and cherry tomatoes are being replaced by leeks and silverbeet. Dorothy stands too long in front of the eggplants. A butchered version of 'Suzanne' plays over the sound system. She'd like to touch one of the eggplants, stroke it, feel how springy and sleek the flesh is, but she's worried about looking like a loony. She is tired by all the impulses she constantly keeps at bay. The lying down on hot asphalt in the middle of the street; the tripping up of small children as they run wobbling towards her; the leaning against the wall in her boss's office and rubbing her face up and down against its bumpy paint. It is the *not* doing of these things that exhausts her. Lying down, particularly, has become a big one. She finds herself wanting to do it all the time, in impossible places – the struggle to stay upright is one she only barely manages to keep winning.

She pushes her trolley, kicking its skewed wheel, through to nuts and grains. The nut dispenser defeats her again and walnuts scatter on the floor. She glances around to check who has noticed her clumsiness. She sees Edward, his back to her, scooping wild rice into a plastic bag. She drops the walnuts again. He hasn't seen, or has pretended not to see, her. Yet. She abandons her trolley and hides behind cereals. It's four months since he moved out. Oh dear. Oh dear oh dear oh dear. This is worse than not good. She is utterly betrayed by her sickening stomach and shaking hands. Until now she had kidded herself that she was over him. 'Suzanne' segues into 'Ain't No Cure for Love.' She hates Leonard Cohen.

What does Edward think when he sees Dorothy spilling walnuts all over the floor? Well, he recognizes her straight away. The curve of her spine as she bends to pick them up – her bad posture – her feet, pointed inwards, that no amount of ballet lessons had ever helped. He feels pity and resentment both at the same time. These are emotions that he has come, over the last six months, to associate with her. Pity that her feet turn inwards; resentment that she has burdened him with her childhood insecurity about this and many other things. He feels a rush of excitement – in the months since he left he has not seen or heard from her and he is curious. He feels claustrophobic. Again.

He busies himself reading the ingredients on a packet of muesli. All those bits of dry, shrivelled fruit and dusty oats. Edward pulls a face. He prefers the toast and coffee approach to breakfast. It's more simple, straightforward, timeless. He doesn't trust people who talk about bran and fibre. How much roughage they're getting. There seems to

him to be something suspicious about having such a fascina-
tion with the inner workings of the body. Dorothy, of course,
would never eat breakfast at all. In one of her frequent fits
of irrationality, she had told him that he made her feel fat.
'It's the way you look at me,' she said, voice wavering. He
didn't tell her it was probably her personality he had an
aversion to, not her waistline. It was near the end. Easier just
to get out, with minimum fuss.

Dorothy avoids him through meat, tinned and dry goods.
Only her feeling that she should be above this stops her
from leaving the supermarket and going home empty-
handed. There ought to be flashbacks, she thinks, postcard
memories of their life together. But all she can remember
now is his face when he told her he was leaving. The sound
of her voice saying, No. No. No no no. The way it's been
four months since she woke up without a hangover. The
time she lit a fire and burned all the books well-meaning
friends had given her – *Women Who Love Too Much, Men
Who Hate Women and the Women Who Love Them, Living
With Solitude*, all the embarrassing, soppy titles. She thinks
of writing her own best-seller, *Women Who Hate the Friends
Who Hate the Men the Women Love*. She remembers some
things. Nice things. Things she doesn't need to remember.
She hates herself for still feeling like she's done something
wrong.

He started off as one of her obsessions. The obsessions
she had that were a joke, to her and to all her friends. She
had these constantly, one or two at a time, lasting for a
week, lasting for six months. Sometimes – in his case –

lasting beyond their usefulness. The obsessions kept her from being bored. They kept her from having to have real relationships. They kept her happily inside the world of romance, where everything is possible except tedium and disgust.

She gave them descriptive names, for easy identification: Mr Bus Stop, Library Man, Glasses, Travis Bickle ('before the mohawk'). Edward began as The Secret, because he was a friend of Martin's and Dorothy didn't want Martin to find out. Even after they'd been openly seeing each other for several months, Dorothy had trouble thinking of him by his real name. On more than one drunken occasion she had been tempted to tell him of his origins, his special place in her world. She always woke up hugely relieved that she had not.

Edward sees her standing by the dairy products, clutching her trolley handle tightly with both hands, rocking almost imperceptibly back and forwards on her heels. He is reminded of how she used to rock sometimes in her chair, at the movies or in front of television. He thinks, my autistic ex-girlfriend. He looks at her white knuckles and remembers how she used to cling to him at night. He'd wake up way over on the edge of the bed, trying to get some breathing space. 'You're so warm,' she'd say. 'It's just because you're so warm.' And other girlfriends had said that too, so he reluctantly believed it. It surprised him – he always thought of himself, with some satisfaction, as a cold-blooded person. It was some strange trick of nature that, at night, naked in bed, he suddenly became warm and gave off heat. He turns away before she can see him looking.

At this stage all Edward really wants to do is to finish his shopping. He wants to fill his trolley, exchange maybe a cordial hello with Dorothy, and go home. To his new home. Which he much prefers. He wants to unpack his groceries and cook dinner and call his friend David. David might come over for a drink. If he thinks about it, Edward might mention Dorothy. 'I saw my ex at the supermarket tonight.' And David will make appropriate, sympathetic noises. They might talk about how irritating it is when a relationship drags on and is hard to finish. They might admit to some guilt about relationships they've ended badly. Or they might not. Edward vaguely imagines this as he wheels back to pick up some pasta. He still thinks he can get out of here unscathed. It's only Dorothy who hears the ticking noise.

Dorothy lingers by the deli section. Maybe he'll walk past as she's expertly checking the date on a Bleu de Bresse. She'll smile winningly at the girl behind the counter, point an elegant finger at the smoked mussels. 'Just a small punnet,' she'll say, 'it's for antipasto.' Edward will stop and wait for her to finish, not wanting to interrupt. 'And I'll need some of that – not too much – oh, Edward!' she'll exclaim, turning around. 'How funny. What a shame I haven't got time to talk properly. You look tired. Must run!' And she'll wheel her delicacies away as he cries, 'Wait! Dorothy – wait—' But he doesn't come past the deli counter, doesn't come near it, and she starts to worry that he might have left the supermarket. She leaves the ricotta and the pickles and the jellied eels, and heads back to where she last saw him.

She fakes bumping into him in the hygiene and toiletries section.

—Hello, Edward, she says, managing to look pleased.

—Oh, hi, Dottie, he says.

She looks at her shoes while he decides whether to stop and talk or to keep on moving down the aisle.

—How are you? he asks.

—*Really* good, she lies, giving herself away more than if she'd told the truth.

She reaches up casually and gets a pack of condoms off the top shelf. She tosses them in her trolley, hating herself, wondering how low she'll stoop in the name of self-preservation. If he notices, he doesn't say anything. Of course.

—I thought you were going away, he says.

—Oh, I was, I am, she says. —Money, you know.

She is affected – she smiles too much. He looks at her bared teeth and is reminded of chimpanzees in body language books. He can't remember if it's fear, or anger, that their smiles express.

—It's always money with you, he says.

She doesn't say anything. She thinks if she breathes in she'll probably cry. Or tell him to fuck himself, which would be temporarily satisfying but destroy any hope she doesn't want to admit she clings to of getting back together.

—Have you seen anyone? I mean, Lucy or Martin? Alannah? How are they?

—They're good, she says. —They ask after you. I told
most people you were drowned at sea.

They both laugh. 'At or with?' she used to say when they
were together. 'Are you laughing at me or with me?' 'It
doesn't matter,' he'd say, and now he feels guilty for letting
her hang over that, over so many things. He puts his hand
on her shoulder.

—Actually no, she says. —No. Don't do that.

—Sorry, he says. Seeing her like this is tiresome, as he
has known it will be. He thinks it would be good to let her
talk, to let her get angry maybe, to make some kind of
atonement.

—Do you want to go for coffee?

—OK, she says quickly. —OK.

Why doesn't he say anything about her hair? He must
have noticed it's a different colour. The week after he left,
she bought a packet of henna. She thought of it as a
therapeutic ritual. She cried as she rubbed the foul-smelling,
gritty paste through her hair. She played the one record he'd
forgotten to take – a scratchy Philip Glass – three times
while she waited for the colour to take. And then she rinsed
the dye off and emerged from under the towel a new
woman. A woman with auburn highlights.

—I'll meet you outside when you've finished.

He wheels his mostly empty trolley over to the check-
out. She wonders if he's cutting his shopping short because
of her, to avoid the awkwardness of meeting around every
corner, forced jollity and tragic one-liners. She wonders if he
needs to shop at all or if he's just come here on Wednesday

night to cruise chicks. She wonders if they'll be able to really talk. She wonders if he wants her back.

At the check-out he wipes his card before putting it back in his pocket. Edward doesn't like strangers touching his things. He doesn't like touching things strangers have touched. He hates the new rubbish bins, the ones with steel flaps that you have to press against to open. They're always cloudy with other people's grease and dirt. He doesn't like pushing the buttons for cross signs, or for lifts. This could be the beginning of a disorder. There are worse disorders. Wanting to avoid other people's germs is probably healthy. Hygienic, anyway. Walking through the automatic doors, he silently praises their inventor.

Dorothy chooses the rest of her groceries carefully, imagining how they'll look to him in their plastic bags. She limits herself to one bottle of wine, better quality than she'd usually buy, thinking she can always come back and get more. Or maybe coffee will turn into a drink and then into dinner, and then maybe—. Maybe. She remembers a holiday they went on together, early in their relationship, to a camping ground. There were bunks in the cabin. They took the mattresses off and slept on the floor. It reminded her of being a kid, staying at friends' houses. The envy she'd felt for those with their own sets of bunks. One friend whose mother always got out the stretcher bed when she stayed the night. They weren't allowed to top and tail in her friend's bed. The same friend told her how she'd walked into the parents' bedroom once and seen them 'doing it', and been so frightened that she ran out of the house and cried. It had made Dorothy feel strange, the stretcher bed, like she had to be put there for her own good. Like she couldn't be trusted.

Outside the supermarket Edward waits while Dorothy finishes her shopping. He thinks of the girl he met last week, the one who gave him her number and said, call me. Call me. He wonders if he still has the number. He can smell the salt and the oil off the harbour. He imagines a movie camera on a crane high above the car park, starting on a wide shot and zooming in to find him, in his black coat, leaning against the wall. He lights a cigarette. Someone comes up to him. A girl he went to high school with, some years ago, in a different city. She has just moved here. She doesn't know anyone. At high school she belonged to a group of girls who used to taunt him, tell everyone he was a faggot, a homo, he didn't like girls. There was something wrong with him. He wonders if she remembers this. It's probably why she's being so nice to him. He tells her where he works, says, call me.

At the check-out Dorothy changes her mind three times about whether or not she'd sleep with him again. She knows it's a battle she's going to lose with herself anyway, so what's the point fighting? She'd like to decide not to though, so if nothing happens at all she can feel like it was her choice. She wonders how bad it would be to read a book with a title like *Smart Women, Foolish Choices*. The teller, a boy with a pony-tail and a pointy noise, tells her she's chosen an excellent wine.

—At least I got something right, she says lamely. She's reduced to banter with a supermarket worker. This is the depth of single-dom. Maybe, given a few months, she'll date someone like this. Who will invariably be too good for her and whose heart she will break. She can't wait. She writes a cheque – no point risking having her card refused – and wheels her shopping slowly toward the exit. She puts a block of cheese in the City Mission trolley, for luck. She's trying to breathe but not hyperventilate. She feels completely alive.

She sees Edward around the corner from the automatic doors, smoking a cigarette, leaning against the fake brick wall. He's talking to someone. It's getting dark outside and for a minute she can't see who it is. Then a car swings its light onto them and she sees a young woman, smiling, drawing her own pack of cigarettes from her coat pocket. Dorothy watches as he laughs at something the girl says and checks his watch. He points at his car. Dorothy's looked for that car nearly every day for the last four months. Every olive green Triumph is like a blow to the solar plexus. Just last week she discussed with a workmate – the new one, who hadn't met Edward and hadn't heard the saga – what useless cars Triumphs were. How only losers drove them. She feels sick. She knows she hasn't got the strength to go up to them, to smile brightly when she is introduced to the girl, to feign enthusiasm when Edward invites the girl to join them for coffee, and to restrain herself from shouting weepy accusations at him across the table.

—Did you hear all the Leonard Cohen in there? the girl from his school asks. —How could they do that?

Edward looks at her blankly. He feels blank. He doesn't

know why he's standing outside a supermarket talking to someone who hated him ten years ago, and waiting for someone who probably hates him now. He sees Dorothy come out of the supermarket. The girl from school is angling for a lift home. He wonders if there's time to drop her off and take Dorothy for coffee without coffee turning into dinner and dinner turning into something more difficult.

Dorothy pulls her trolley back around the corner and pushes it the six blocks home, like a little girl with a pram that's too big for her. If anyone stops her she'll scream at them.

Edward looks over to the doors again and sees the wheels of Dorothy's trolley backing into the shadows around the corner. He doesn't know what she's playing at. He excuses himself from the other girl and goes around the corner to watch Dorothy pushing her shopping quickly down the road, back straight now but feet still pigeon-toed. He says, forget it. Forget it. He walks back to his car. The girl from school is gone. He fumbles, going for his car keys, and they fall out of his hands and down a dirty drain in the pavement, full with water and butts and scum.

How does he remember the moment? The beginning of them, together? If asked, he'll probably say he doesn't. Understandable – the forgetting, the deleting, or the merging of many moments into one. Ask me something important, he'll say, like how it was when he crashed his car, or lost his virginity, or took acid, or stepped for the first time off a plane and into another country. But Dorothy? Well. The truth is that he does remember a version of it, dimly.

Something involving many bottles of wine. Something involving mutual friends. Something involving a feeling that she discovered him, not the other way around. A feeling of unease. A feeling that he didn't mind unease. That's enough, he says. Leave it that way, he says.

When Dorothy gets to her house she empties the trolley and gives it a really good push halfway down her street. A car pulls out just in time to be hit in the side by the ghost trolley, which leaves a thin scratch down the paintwork. She bolts her door and turns off all the lights in the house. She curls up on the floor in the hallway and imagines Edward waiting and waiting for her to come out of the supermarket, and wonders how long it took before he decided to leave.

# *thinking about sleep*

They're not going to let us all see Robert. None of us are family, and it seems when somebody hits the ground with that big a crunch, the results can be pretty gruesome. There's some talk from the people behind the desk. Robert's blood family are out of the country and no one has got hold of them. Somebody needs to identify the body now. The one wearing glasses asks Maria how long she's been living with him.

—Two and a half years, she says, —three maybe.

The hospital people flick through some forms.

—OK, the glasses one says. —That's de facto I suppose. Come with me, please.

So the three of us wait while Maria follows the man down the long corridor and into a lift. I can't quite see the numbered lights above the lift, but I imagine when it gets to Maria's stop it's glowing a little orange M.

It's a long time to wait. None of us move from where we're standing. I don't want to look at anyone so I look mostly at the floor. The lino's very shiny and slippery looking, apart from the bit under our feet which is scraped and scratched, like a little worn island in the middle of the polish.

—There's been a mistake, says Toby. —We shouldn't have come here.

—We can't leave now, says Martin.

An orderly in a green coat wheels a trolley of food past us. It smells like knuckles in gravy. I feel sick. Toby lights a cigarette.

—For fuck's sake, Tobe, says Martin, too loud.

Toby looks stricken. He laughs, sheepishly. —Sorry, he says. —I forgot.

He puts his cigarette out in a pot plant. I want to hug him.

After a few more minutes the lift doors open and Maria steps out into the corridor. It's as bad as anything's ever been, standing here by the desk, watching her walk slowly down towards us. She walks very close to the wall but she doesn't reach out and touch it. It seems like for ever and now she's with us, not looking, looking at the pot plant.

—He's OK, she says. —I mean, he's dead, it's him.

She breathes in really fast, like a sob, and Martin steps forward to hold her. Her legs buckle, she goes broken in his arms, and he leans against the desk for support. They slide down it until they're sitting on the floor, Maria's whole back going up and down, up and down as she takes in sharp scary breaths. I can't think of anything. I can't think of anything. I see Maria down in the basement for all those minutes with Robert's body. I can't comprehend it. It's so big it fills up my head and I push through the glass doors to get outside. Next thing, I'm dry retching over the gravel where the cars turn around. I straighten up for some air and see Maria scramble to her feet and run after me. She's here and she hugs me and we stay like this until we're both breathing more or less normally. Her fingers are entangled in my hair, clutching it, clutching me to her. She presses her cheek against mine. Although I feel like I'm burning up, her face is totally cold.

Toby and Martin are outside now too. Toby's sucking on another cigarette. Martin has his hands in his pockets, stamping softly on the gravel. I realize in half an hour it will be dark. I breathe. I just concentrate on breathing.

—I don't want to go home, says Maria, her voice hoarse.

—Come to our house, says Martin. —Kate? You come too. I think Lucy will be there.

—OK, I say. —I'll come.

I can see our breath clouding the air in front of us. Us all standing here in the cold, Toby, Martin, Maria and me. No one else.

Toby says he'll bring the car round.

—I'll walk, I say.

—Are you sure? says Martin.

—Yeah, I'd like to.

Maria holds my hand. She takes something out of her coat pocket and puts it in mine.

—You have this, she says. —I might want it later but I don't want it now.

I kiss her and leave them there, Martin and Toby with

their arms around each other, Maria small and white beside them.

It takes a while to walk through the industrial area that separates the hospital from the suburb where we live. The buildings are all closed up and silent. I remember that it's a Sunday. The street lights go on. I can hear a dog barking. The last time I saw Robert was at a party at his and Maria's place two weeks ago. Most people had gone home. Maria was in bed, and Robert and Lucy and I sat up, finishing a bottle and playing cards, the mess from the party all around us. A Frank Sinatra record was on, and when 'Something Stupid' started Robert turned the volume up as loud as it could go. He grabbed Lucy and they sang it together, using empty bottles as microphones, making silly big-eye faces and laughing. The song finished and they kissed. I clapped. I turned around and saw Maria in the doorway, in her underwear, her hair sticking out all over the place.

—Come to bed, Robert, she said.

Lucy left. I slept on the couch for a couple of hours, too drunk or too tired or too something to go home. The next day, Robert disappeared. He didn't have his medication with him.

When I get to Toby and Martin's everyone else is already there. Toby gives me a glass of red wine.

—Where's Maria? I say.

—She's asleep, says Martin. He squeezes my arm. — Lucy's in the kitchen.

I go in and find her chopping onions. The kitchen's full of the sharp smell of them.

—Hey, Luce, I say. I hug her and she hugs me back but in a brave hard way, like she doesn't want to talk about it.

—Hi, Kate, she says. —I'm cooking. Do you want some?

—I don't know, I say. —Maybe.

I stand by the window and look at the dark wintery garden. Robert's dead, I think. Robert's dead. I'm about to try saying it out loud when one of the shadows in the garden moves towards the kitchen door.

—Lucy, I whisper. —Lucy—. I want to cry.

—It's Frank, she says, —he's been out there since we heard. He thinks he's weeding.

Frank comes in the door. His hands and knees have black dirt all over them. He smells of the earth and the cold.

—Katie, he says, smiling at me. —Hey.

He touches my face and frowns. He looks down at his hands.

—Oh, he says. —I got a mark on you.

—It's OK, I say. —But you better go and wash.

—Its cold out there, he says. He leans over and whispers in my ear. —If this is *The Big Chill*, I don't want to be William Hurt.

—Fuck off, Frank, I say. —Fuck right off. You're disgusting. He goes into the living room, where Toby and Martin are drinking.

—What did he say? says Lucy.

—Nothing, I say, —you don't want to know.

—I can't deal with his way of dealing with this, says Lucy. —I know it sounds selfish but it's just too much. We nearly had a fight but Martin stopped it. I can't remember what it was about.

There's a pause. Then she says, —Did you see him?

—No, I say. —Just Maria.

—Isn't someone supposed to be organizing everything? What about all that? What about his family?

—I don't know, I say, and I realize that I don't. —Maybe tomorrow.

—God, his family, she says.

I think of Robert's parents sitting together on the plane back home. Having heard the news, having had to leave wherever they are and change their tickets and pack their bags. Sitting tightly together on the plane. Lost in the air. I wish I hadn't thought of them. Robert's mother, Robert's father.

—Why am I chopping onions? Lucy puts the knife down. —What am I doing? Am I cooking? What am I cooking?

—Just leave it, I say, holding her wine glass out to her. —Come and sit down.

She's crying. —Oh, these fucking onions, she says.

—Yeah, I say, and I laugh, —it's really the onions.

She laughs too. She sits down on the floor like Maria at the hospital and we laugh the way you do when you're getting too much oxygen and you cry as well and you make those funny moan noises when you try and stop. Eventually we do stop. The laughing leaves us, with a few last shuddery breaths. I have a bitter taste in my mouth.

—Kate I don't know what to do, says Lucy. —I just don't know what to do.

—I don't know who does, I say. I shut my eyes. Everything hurts. —I'm going to have to go home.

—Can you take Frank? I can't—.

—Sure.

—How could Robert do this to Maria? Lucy's voice gets hard. —How could he do this?

I can't think of anything to say. I still think Robert must have made a mistake somehow. I can't, just can't understand it. I want an injection, or a blow to the head. Anything. I can't think about it any more.

—Is Maria staying here?

—Yeah, says Lucy. —Martin and Toby'll look after her.

—Good, I say. —Call me later.

We join the others. Toby's a little drunk, unsteady on his feet, his face streaky. Martin looks impassive, broad-shouldered, old.

I say, —Frank, you're coming with me.

—OK. He gets up and puts his coat on like a little boy. We all say careful, frightened goodbyes. Lucy starts crying again when she hugs me. Everyone looks tired and drawn, and I'm struck by how beautiful they all are. We exchange kisses and let go of each other slowly and reluctantly.

On the way home Frank doesn't talk. He sings a funny little Irish song about a fisherman. I think it's supposed to cheer us up but the minor key doesn't help and I have to tell him to be quiet. We get to my door.

—Kate, says Frank. —Katie Katie Kate.

—All right, I say, —I don't want to be alone either.

Inside, I get Frank a blanket. When I put it round his

shoulders he starts shaking. He shakes and shakes. I hold
him and stroke his bony back.

—Fuck it, he says. —Fuck it.

I make some tea. It stops his teeth chattering. He still has
dirt under his fingernails.

—It's going to be OK, I say.

—Don't lie, he says.

He tells me about a fight he had with Robert once. Robert
had been away and Frank slept with Maria. She told Robert
when he got back and he went straight over to Frank's. They
pushed each other around a bit and then, Frank says, they
started saying things. Stupid things you mean at the time
but you can't stand to think about later. Things you can't
forget. I can't believe Frank. I can't believe Maria either. It
is the lowest possible thing, that they both deceived Robert
like that. I try to remember the time he's talking about, if
there was anything about it that makes sense now. Robert
away. Where had he even gone? Jesus. I suppose Frank and
Maria had their reasons. Robert had his reasons too. But he
was faithful to Maria the whole time they were together. I
know. I didn't ask for it to be that way, but Robert was
faithful. A couple of months after the thing with Frank,
Robert got depressed. It can't have been for the first time
but it was the first time any of us knew about it. I remember.
Maria told me the doctor had given him some pills. She was
frightened. She didn't know what it meant. She said the one
good thing was, he wasn't drinking.

—Frank it's not your fault Robert got sick, I say.

—I know, he says, pushing his teacup away. —It just feels like it, that's all.

I know I should be more understanding, but I get angry.

—Get over it, Frank, I say. —This isn't about you.

—It's about all of us Kate, he says. —And you're stupid if you can't see that. What do you think, Robert's off a bridge and that's not about you?

—Fuck you, Frank, I say. —Robert just made some dumb fucking mistake, he didn't take a pill or he took one fucking pill too many, I don't know, he slipped, whatever, don't you dare—

—Sshh, says Frank, —don't yell.

—I'll yell in my own fucking house if I want to, Frank, I say, quietly. —I don't want to have this fight. I'm going for a walk.

Outside, the temperature has dropped right down and the moon is skinny and pale. I start walking fast and dig my hands deep into my pockets to keep warm. I feel what I think is a crumpled bit of paper. I stop. I remember what Maria gave me. My throat's tight and there's a thudding in my gut. I can't believe it. I can't believe what I have. What I've been carrying around with me since the hospital, what now feels like it's scorching a hole in my coat, what's going to make everything clear. I leave the note in my pocket and run, down my street, through the park, across roads and around corners, past the shops until I'm standing at the road that goes left to the motorway bridge and right to the pipe. The pipe.

There was one time when Robert and I went for a walk along the pipe. It's a big thing, about four feet across, that runs over the lagoon by the sea. It goes for ages and though it's wide enough to walk along comfortably, my sense of balance is bad and I always feel mildly panicked on it. It takes a good twenty minutes to walk it and the sensation's something like having claustrophobia and vertigo at the same time. I don't know why I was walking it with Robert this day. We might have been on our way to or from somewhere. Or it might just have been a walk, back in those months when we used to take walks together. I remember walking behind Robert, not liking the feeling that I was trailing after him, but liking being able to look at his back, his hair, his legs. About half-way across we stayed still for a minute. It smelled like rain and the greyness of the sky and the pipe and the lagoon made me feel more confused. Robert's hand brushed against mine. I thought it was an accident but then he took my hand and held it. Normally I would have got as far away from him as I could but the lagoon was in front of me and behind me and the pipe offered no escape at all. So I moved closer to him, into his big soft enveloping jersey. I think we stood like that for a while.

I think about that day on the pipe all the way along the road towards the bridge. When I get there the thin cold air burns into the back of my throat. I hold my hands over my ears. I shut my eyes. I open them and the world is still there. I lean against the bridge, gasping. As I walk along it I make myself look down over the edge. Bits of police ribbon are still flapping on the ground down there, rigged up between those reflector stick things. If I could climb down there and lie where he's lain, down there on the asphalt where his body has been, I don't think I'd be able to leave. I'm so afraid of forgetting him, so afraid of feeling anything less confused than I'm feeling now, of being rational about something that it doesn't seem fair to ever be rational about, that I could go down there and lie on that asphalt and eat the loose stones that his head has fallen on.

Instead I stare at the place until my eyes water and I think I have it printed on the back of my skull. I reach into my pocket for the note. I can't feel anything there. It must have fallen out when I was running. I can't breathe. I shove my hands into all my pockets, my coat, my jeans. I rip the lining of my coat, I throw it on the ground and fall on it, scrabbling, unable to believe the note is gone. Two kids run past me, zigzagging from one side of the bridge to the other. I curl up on my coat and don't lift my head until I can't hear them any more. I look up at the dark sky and ask anything out there to please give me the note back, please, please. I make promises I'll never remember again. I'll do anything, I say, anything you want.

And it comes blowing down the street towards me, a small screwed-up bit of paper that at this moment I want more than my life. I crawl towards it. It blows a bit closer. The wind picks up and I think I've lost it forever and it feels like punishment for every sin I've ever committed. Then it's in my hands and I clutch it to me as hard as I can. I smoothe it out, trying not to let go of any part of it. The streetlights are dim and it's hard to see clearly. I blink and squint and hold it so there's no shadow falling on it. I read,

I'm sorry. I don't mean for it to be this way.

R.

There's nothing else. I don't know what I think. It's the answer to a question but it's not the answer that I want. The note looks small, extremely small and as crumpled and tired and sweat-stained and pathetic as I feel. Robert held this paper. They must have found it on him. And they'd given it to Maria and she'd given it to me. This small tired last thing of Robert's. Which I have to hold on to as if it means something.

The walk home seems shorter than it took to get to the bridge. For a couple of confused minutes everything looks unfamiliar and I think I must be lost. I can't tell where some shapes begin and others end. Then I see my house, standing third along from the bend in the street like it always does. I can't understand how it looks so different to me, as if I'm approaching it from a new place or a part of town I've never been in before. It could be me, not everyone else, who's been to sleep, and during my dreams years have passed and the street has changed and whole families have moved in and out of my house – nobody knowing that I've lived there or that I might one day come back to it.

Robert rang me one Christmas when he was away, just to hear a friendly voice, he said, just to picture me there in my house talking to him. Tell me how the kitchen looks, he said, and the garden. And you. I clutched those words to me for a long time after. Robert. His big shoulders, his laugh. What going to a beach with him was like, or a gallery, a park, even just the movies. Everything looked different when you were there with him. Brighter colours. Or was this just me, the way I worked when he was there? I know it wasn't always like that for him. Maria shouted at me once, You don't have him seven days a week. You don't know what it's like. She knew, about a lot of things.

I haven't got my key. I sit on the doorstep. I must have made a noise, because Frank opens the door.

—Are you OK? he says.

—I didn't think you'd be here.

—You're freezing.

We sit on the couch and he puts his arms around me. We sort of fumble against each other. I'm shocked by the smoothness of his skin. But it's not about that, what we want, so we stop.

—Where did you go? he says.

—Nowhere. Can I have a cup of tea?

—Look at you, he says. —You're so tired.

I let him steer me into my bedroom. I lie down on the bed and he takes my shoes and socks off for me. That makes me cry.

—Frank, I say, —can you stay?

And so we lie curved against each other under about five blankets, thinking about sleep while the room gets lighter.

I imagine Maria waking up, standing in the doorway with her underwear on and her hair sticking out all over the place, and realizing that he still isn't here.

I imagine the place under the bridge, and can't remember if the colour of the police cordon is yellow or blue.

I imagine turning my head around and seeing Robert's face instead of Frank's pressing into my shoulder.

The wind outside makes the curtains move even though the windows are shut.

Not even the first twenty-four hours without him are over, I think. Less than a whole day out of somebody's life.

# some common mistakes

Cherry stands naked in front of the mirror and has a good look. She's fat. Her legs, her arms, her bum, her stomach – all of it is fat. She puts her jeans and T-shirt on again, slowly. She decides she looks best either completely naked or completely clothed. Half undressed makes her look bulgy in the wrong places.

She picks up her thin light yellow hair and pulls it hard. A few hairs come out in her hands but not many. She sits at her dressing table and stares into the magnifying mirror above it. Without taking her eyes off her eyes, she leans forward and picks up the kitchen snips. She raises them to her hairline just above her ear. She cuts at the air and the scissors make a grunting noise. She grabs the long wispy hair at the top of her head and cuts it right off, holding the snips as close to her scalp as she can. She slowly works around her whole head like this. Her arm gets sore but she ignores it. Her face and hands are covered with strands of dead hair. It tickles but she's not allowed to brush it away. She's not allowed to do anything until it's all gone.

Soon she's got no hair left to cut. Her scalp is naked except for a layer of short fine bristles. When it was long her hair had been a kind of grubby blonde. Now it's almost transparent, a beige non-colour hair that blends in with her skin. She looks a bit like a war refugee. She smudges kohl under her eyes to compound the effect. She sucks her cheeks in.

—

Later in the day, Warren arrives. Warren is Cherry's ex. You're my ex, she always wants to say to him, but never does. There's no reason for wanting to say it apart from how much she likes the word. Ex ex ex. She can say it with her chin jutting out. They've been broken up for three months now, but Warren still comes over most days in his lunch hour. It's very important for Warren to know that he can still screw Cherry (screw, that's his word for it, feel like a screw, Cherry?) even though they're not together any more. Cherry understands this. Warren says there's nothing wrong with screwing Tricia, his new girlfriend, but sometimes during the day he just needs a bit extra, and Tricia only gets half an hour for lunch, plus she works on the other side of town, so what can he do? Warren's a tech drawing teacher at the local high school.

Cherry hasn't minded still fucking Warren. She comes almost as soon as he touches her down there. She gets turned on by anything a little bit dirty, and Cherry thinks sex is really, really dirty. Especially now that she and Warren don't go out together. She gets so turned on by how dirty it is that she can spend the whole morning in a trance just thinking about it. It's not as if Warren's good looking either. He's got clumsy fat hands and sometimes he doesn't wash properly. Cherry loves it.

It takes a while for Warren to get over the shock of Cherry's new look.

—Fuck, he says, —what happened to ya hair?

He's in a pissy mood. He had to stop Tony Mune and Donna Prescott from pashing up in the quad before school. All the third formers could see them, for Christ's sake, and there she was with her too-short school uniform hitched up even further, and there he was with his big sixteen-year-old knee shoved in between hers, ridiculous in his grey shorts. It pissed Warren off, he tells Cherry, while she undoes his belt and pulls his trousers down. He doesn't say that what made him even angrier were the slow, smug smiles they both gave him as he prised them apart, looking at him as if they knew exactly what he wanted and that he couldn't have it. Bloody no respect. That smile was what got Tony Mune the extra detention, not the softly drawled 'wanker' that Warren overheard as he walked away.

Cherry lifts up one of his feet and yanks the shoe off. The trouser leg follows.

—No, Cherry, come on. What the fuck happened?

She's got the other shoe off now and she stands and looks at him, worried in his yellow jockeys and his jacket and shirt. She pulls his jocks off. She likes the way he looks now. She imagines him reading the news like that, suit on top, birthday suit below.

—Did ya have a fight with the lawn-mower? Cherry?

—I cut it, she says, walking into the kitchen.

Cherry makes Warren keep his shirt and jacket on while they do it on the kitchen floor. The lino's cold and hard and Warren complains about it. They roll over so he's on top. Cherry grabs the fish-slice off the floor and hits Warren on the bum with it. He screams. She's going for it today.

Cherry refuses to get off the floor while Warren dresses.

—You can see yourself out, she says. —Have a nice afternoon.

—Cherry . . . do you want to go to the movies this week?

—No, thanks, Warren. Bye.

Warren looks at her for a while and then he leaves. Cherry stays on the kitchen floor until it gets dark.

———

The next day Cherry gets up late. She does her eye make-up again so she looks malnourished. She adds some shadows under her cheekbones for good measure. She holds her stomach in and stretches her arms above her head so she can count her ribs.

She colours in her nipples with lipstick and goes to collect the mail naked.

Outside is very cold and Cherry's skin puckers into goosebumps. The mail hasn't arrived yet so Cherry stands by the gate waiting for the postie. The street is quiet. She pushes the bell chained to the gate back and forth. It makes a small dull metal noise. Cherry doesn't know what she's going to do when the postie arrives. She decides to take her

cue from him. Her feet are freezing. She goes inside to put
socks on, then runs back out to the gate.

The postie walks past pushing his bike.

—Any mail?' asks Cherry.

—Not today, he says.

—What's your name? says Cherry.

—Malcolm, he answers, turning to look at her. —What's
yours?

—Cherry.

—Well, Cherry, you'll catch your death out here with
nothing on.

—Oh, yeah. Thanks.

Cherry walks back into the house. She shuts the door and
turns the heating up.

When Warren comes to visit she doesn't answer the door.
He knocks for a long time. She can hear him cursing. She
doesn't care. She's watching Oprah.

Cherry has made a decision about Warren. She's decided
to make him go this whole week without sex. She didn't like
him asking her to the movies like that. She's afraid he wants
something from her. Also, she's decided that it's not fair on
Tricia. Cherry thinks she might quite like Tricia.

She rang Tricia's house one night to see how she would
respond to a silent phone call. This is Cherry's way of
assessing the characters of people she doesn't know very
well. She is sure that it's a foolproof method. When she'd
first started going out with Warren she rang him anony-
mously at least three times a night to see what reaction he
would have. At first he'd just hung up when he didn't hear

anyone talking, but Cherry persisted. After a while he became abusive. Cherry was surprised and intrigued to hear the kind of language that he knew. Disappointingly, he didn't use it with very much imagination. That's when Cherry knew it would be a fairly short affair.

—Hello? said Tricia the first time Cherry called. —Excuse me? Beg pardon? Anybody there?

Then Tricia just hung up. Cherry called back fifteen minutes later and nearly got her ear-drum destroyed by the piercing whistle Tricia blew down the phone. Cherry was shaken but impressed. Since then she's been worried about how Tricia would feel if she knew Warren was still coming to her house for sex. Cherry suspects that Tricia wouldn't put up with it, and might even break up with Warren. Then he'd probably want Cherry back. She feels tired just thinking about it. So it seems best if Warren just doesn't come around for a while. He'll get the picture soon enough.

She spends the evening painting her nails and removing the polish, until all her colours run out.

—

Tricia didn't come home till two this morning. She spent half an hour throwing up with the bathroom door open so Warren could hear everything, and then climbed into bed still drunk.

She lies in their waterbed feeling seasick and thinking about the lump in her jaw. It has to be cancer. When she was little the next-door neighbour had jaw cancer. Tricia was disgusted by how ugly the woman looked after her operation. Her parents used this as an example of what would happen to Tricia if she ever started smoking. She took it up at fifteen anyway, and now this lump was a physical punishment for her lack of compassion towards the neighbour. It didn't matter that she gave smoking up a year ago because of the nasty wrinkles that were appearing around her eyes. It was going to be her fate to suffer the same post-surgical disfiguration, her fate to frighten small children in the street.

Warren's reaction to Tricia's announcement that she is probably going to have her jaw amputated has not been at all satisfactory. He barely seems to notice. His only concession has been to leave her alone when she complained that kissing hurt. Perhaps if she complains more he will go and sleep in the lounge. He's been threatening to do this for a fortnight anyway. She wouldn't care. Goodness me, no. She knows all this is a sign that she should do something, i.e. hiff Warren, but she really doesn't want to be both cancerous and single.

—

When Cherry tries to get out of bed she falls over. She lies on the floor surprised. The edges of her vision are blurry and black. This must be a side-effect of her diet. Maybe it is too extreme to completely cut out food altogether. But it's something to do, starve. It occupies her day. She thinks about food and then she thinks about eating it. She thinks about being fat and she thinks about being thin. She looks in the mirror. Fat. She looks in the cupboard. Bare. She thinks about buying some food just so she can have it there as a temptation to resist. She writes lists of fat food and lists of thin food. Fat: butter, cream, eggs, chocolate, chips. Thin: rice crackers, water. She drinks a lot of water. Sometimes when she drinks it she imagines it is soup, or a milkshake. Mmm, thick and creamy, filling up her mouth. This should work. The imagination diet.

Exercise is important as well, so Cherry religiously follows the aerobics classes on television. Sometimes she has lots of energy and she jumps up and down in front of the TV, twice as high and twice as fast as the pastel leotard instructors. Other times she is far too tired to participate, but watches anyway. There's a t'ai chi class on afterwards. This makes her laugh. Turn to the south, and push. She tries this but it is too slow for her to keep her balance and she falls down again. Getting up, falling down, thinking about food, not eating. Along with the little sleeps she has to take every three hours or so this is quite an easy way to make the day go by.

—

A result of the jaw lump is Tricia's diminishing sense of confidence in her attractiveness to men. She still likes to go out with the girls to their favourite wine bar, but flirting with the barman is not the same when you know you're about to suffer a premature and ugly death. She feels very alone in her anxiety. It's too hard to explain all this to Warren, and she certainly can't explain it to the girls. Oh, they'd sympathize all right, but it might give one or two of them some bright ideas – they might think they could move in on her turf – and Warren, she fears, is somewhat vulnerable to feminine attention. No, at this stage it is definitely for the best if she keeps her worries to herself. It is the most dignified approach, and Tricia thinks a dignified and tragic ending may well be the way to go. Anyway, she doesn't know for sure yet what her diagnosis is – she hasn't dared go to the doctor. She's still living for the future. It might be quite nice to get a little kitten, actually. And today's a good day to wash her hair. Oh, she feels better already. Brave girl.

—

Warren rings Cherry up. He doesn't say he wants to come round straight away. He tells her about how fucked things are at his school, how all their tech drawing equipment dates back to 1976, how he's not speaking to the head of his department and how they've made the staff room non-smoking. Jesus, Cherry, he says, it's a mug's game. And when I read someone whinging on in the paper about how teachers have such a cushy deal with holidays every three months I just get bloody furious. Cherry? Cherry is studying her toenails. They are getting smaller and wrinkled, like her mother's.

—Cherry? I might just pop round? You think?
Cherry sighs. —No, thanks, Warren.
—Well, we don't have to – I mean I'd just like to talk.
—You're talking to me now, Warren, says Cherry.
—Yeah, but.

Cherry wonders if she can put her little toe in her mouth without dropping the telephone. She discovers that she can't. She drops the telephone. Warren's voice mutters on for a bit more, tinny and small from the floor, until he hangs up. Cherry can count her ribs now without having to stretch upwards. She shadows under each one of them very carefully. Grey under her eyes, under her cheekbones, and under her ribs. There's a nice birdcage effect happening below her collarbone. Good. This is all good. She lifts her arms out to the side and rotates her wrists. She's getting lighter. Soon she'll be able to lift off.

—

Tricia goes to the dentist. This is a peculiar experience, mainly because of the curious sexual attraction she finds herself feeling for him. She watches his hands as much as she can when they are out of her mouth, and when he says open wide she doesn't mind at all. He slips an injection into her gum so gently that she doesn't know he's done it.

He says —You've got a nasty abccess, look at this lump.

She's embarrassed, as if he's pointing out she hasn't washed properly. Then she realizes – can it be? – he is talking about her cancer.

—A dead tooth by the look of it. Feel anything when I do this?

She looks at him misty-eyed. No, she feels nothing. A dead tooth. No jaw surgery. No cancer.

—Are oo aw? she asks him.

—Uh? Yep, hasn't this been hurting? Whole nerve must be gone. No problem, I'll just fill it right up. Do it now if you like.

And she lies back and closes her eyes while the man who has saved her from ugliness drills into her mouth. The smell of burning tooth that usually makes her think of horrible dead things now smells like life. Pretty Tricia's pretty life.

The dentist's office is on the sixth floor of a modern building. Two window cleaners swing past in their hanging contraption. The dentist takes his hands away from Tricia's mouth. She opens her eyes. He goes to the window and pulls down the blinds.

—Don't want them watching do we?

For a minute she thinks he's really going to try something. This is not nice. It's one thing her lying back in this chair having fantasies but it's quite another thing him taking advantage. She crosses her ankles, and is relieved when he picks up the drill and asks her to rinse out again.

After he's fixed her teeth she looks in the mirror and the full strength of her beauty thrills her. She touches her jaw carefully and feels almost fond of the lump, now benign, that will slowly recede from her face. She smiles at him through the Novocaine, a beautiful Bells palsy half-numb smile. Dentists are very well paid, aren't they? And so clean.

And then, when she gets home, all ready to hiff Warren, he tells her that he loves her. He's sitting on the couch clutching a bottle.

—I love you, Trish, he says, in a voice she's only ever heard him use when his team have won the cricket, full of sentiment and beer. —I just want you to know that. I really, really love you, Tricia, you're the best – the best—.

Well, of course, she can't leave him now. How could she leave him now? He's laid himself bare to her. He loves her. She loves him too.

—

Cherry wakes up. She stands up. Again the floor looks like it's coming up to meet her. She falls back onto the bed. Her head hits the corner of a box that's somehow on the bed too. She's out again.

And so there's a headache, and there's dry retching over the toilet bowl, which may or may not be for other reasons, and there's a very strong feeling that the world is conspiring against her. She leans her head against the bathroom wall and falls asleep again. When she wakes up from not dreaming she rinses her mouth out. She misses Warren. He used to rinse her mouth out for her.

She plays patience. Before it came to this she despised herself when she played patience. It seemed like the most wasteful waste of time there was. Now she loves it, loves the mindless flipping over of cards, three on three on three until there's something she can move. Now it seems like the perfect use of her time. She still resists it, sits looking at the pack of cards for long minutes before she allows herself to pick them up and place them down. Then she plays game after game until she loses herself in the pattern of the cards on the floor and the rhythm of the cards in her hand. She doesn't have to count out seven across anymore. It's automatic. It's automatic seeing where the cards will go, if there's a place for them to move to or not. Seeing as each new card is turned up if it has its partner waiting for it on the floor, ready for it to be laid in place and continue the chain down.

—

Now that she and Warren are in love, Tricia thinks it might be worth giving him some gentle advice on his wardrobe. She brings home catalogues for postal-order clothing companies and leaves them out on the table. When, a day later, Warren hasn't said anything, Tricia circles some of the nicer outfits and lays the leaflets on their bed. Still nothing. Tricia is in a quandary. It's all right to drop hints about these things – the way she has about his personal hygiene, buying Listerine and maximum-strength deodorant in the super-market shopping – but his fashion sense is too delicate a subject for her to just come right out and criticize. Perhaps she'll buy him a little present. A new tie, maybe. New socks at the very least. She looks at his sans-a-belts hanging in the wardrobe and sighs. His corduroy jacket makes her want to weep. Oh Warren, Warren, if only you had taste. Then he would truly be the Perfect Man. She imagines him in a polo shirt at the wheel of a boat, cotton trou and loafers, casual but smart. A haircut. Some highlights maybe, like George Michael. New aftershave. She has managed to get rid of the Brut 33, discreetly tipping small amounts down the basin every night until it's gone. This image revamp is going to take some time. Well, she does love him. She's in for the long haul.

—

It's Cherry's reporting day at the Labour Department. This will be her first venture out of the house since she went to get the mail naked. She dresses in baggy clothes that hide how fat she is. She hunts the house for a pair of sunglasses to wear but can't find any. Would it be too much to wear a bag over her head? She remembers the signs in the Labour Department, like the signs in a bank, saying Wearing of Crash Helmets Not Allowed. Probably a paper bag is out of the question.

There's a letter in the letter-box. It's not for her. It's been delivered to the wrong address.

On the bus into town an old man who smells sits down next to her. His smell is of sweat, urine and methylated spirits. Cherry almost gags. She sits turned completely away from him. Why is it always the freaks that sit next to me? she thinks. Why must I be singled out by these beggars? Two years ago, in what seems now like her other life, she went to India. Every amputee seemed to call her name, every blind man's hand seemed to stretch out for her. She was horrified by it in the way you are horrified by something you recognize as utterly familiar. She didn't know how to deal with it. She took a lot of drugs. But once she'd realized she was a freak magnet, the idea followed her back home and has been impossible to escape. She can't take her eyes off a spastic person in the street, even though she's been told it's rude to stare. She's enthralled by how close she is to that twitching uncontrol herself. Seeing it makes her feel the keenness of the knife-edge she walks between normality and freakdom. How easy to let your limbs flail out in front of the world, how easy to scream in church or throw a shoe at the movie screen. She knows how close she is to the threshold. She also knows how often she longs to cross it.

She queues at the Labour Department like everyone else, after looking at the job cards on the notice-boards as if she's interested.

—Got your form? says the lady at the desk.

Cherry hands it over to be signed.

—Nothing there I'm qualified for.

The woman looks at Cherry as if she's heard it all before..

—Is this a good job? Cherry asks.

—Which one's that then.

—Yours.

—Oh. Well, yes, yes, it is.

—Why don't you let someone else have a go? says Cherry.

—Next please, says the woman, tidying the papers on her desk.

Cherry has found that by using a direct attack like this she prevents them noticing the Long-Term Unemployed she now has stamped on her form. Two years doesn't seem that long-term to Cherry, but the Department make their own distinctions. She dreads the phone call that will ask her to come in for an assessment, or take part in a re-training course. How to put a CV together. How to dress for an interview. What not to do. Ten common mistakes. If they're so common, why don't they stop calling them mistakes? Cherry makes at least ten mistakes every day, probably more. Cherry is a mistake, according to her mother, and as such should surely be granted exemption from these courses, which after all work on the assumption that people believe mistakes are bad, and want to be told how to stop making them.

Her head is cold. Freezing. It must be this dumb haircut. She goes past a hairdressers and asks them if they've got any wigs she can try on. They bring out a selection of cheap nylon wigs, like dead animals thinks Cherry as she places each one experimentally on her head. She looks unbalanced somehow – the hair too big for her body.

—These are all too big, she tells the hairdresser.

—It's because you're such a skinny thing, dear, he says.

She looks at him. —No, I'm not. I'm gross. What's wrong with your eyes?

Cherry walks home from town. The exercise is a good idea. And it saves her the bus fare. She can't walk very fast these days so it takes a while. She imagines she's a secretary strolling home after a hard day at the office. When she gets home she'll call her friend Amanda who works for Hewlett Packard. They'll swap gossip about their bosses and advice on fingernail maintenance. Then her fiancé will pick her up and take her back to his de luxe apartment and they'll do it all night and he'll bring her breakfast in the morning, only grapefruit thanks, Bruce, I'm on a diet—.

When she reaches her real home, hot and sweaty, the phone is ringing. It stops before she can pick it up. She spends the evening lip-synching in the mirror to her old Pretenders records.

—

A sweet little kitty, Tricia decides. A gift of love from her to Warren. But it'll be hers really, a pretty little girl cat to play games with and spoil with special tidbits. Fluffy and white, with mischievous blue eyes. She's looking under Pet Shops in the Yellow Pages when the phone rings.

—Hello? says Tricia, —hello?

Cherry holds the receiver tightly and doesn't breathe.

—Cherry, says Tricia, —is that you?

Cherry bites her fingers.

—I know it's you, says Tricia, —and you can't have him. Do you hear me? Over my dead body.

They both hang up at the same time.

An hour passes. Cherry calls again. The phone rings and rings and she waits and waits. She sits there for so long she forgets what she's doing, until suddenly she hears Tricia pick up.

—Yes? says Tricia, furious.

Cherry says nothing. She puts a hand over her mouth as if demonstrating to a child to be quiet.

Tricia screams. —Leper!

The phone slams.

Cherry is so stunned that she can't put the receiver down. She holds it to her, rubs it over her face, hugs it like a baby as tears form in her eyes.

—

Warren gets home from parent–teacher interviews to find Tricia putting make-up on.

—You look nice. Where are you going?

—Out.

—Oh. Want a drink?

—No, thank you.

Warren gets himself a beer.

—Jeez the kids were little shits today. Some of their parents, boy, you can see why. Asking me why their kid isn't doing better in TD when they're as thick as two short planks themselves. What the fuck do they expect, you know?

Tricia brushes her hair and sprays perfume into her cleavage.

Warren stands behind her and puts his arms around her waist. He bites her neck. She elbows him in the ribs.

—Not now, please, Warren.

—Jesus, Tricia, what's the matter?

—Nothing's the matter, I just don't feel like it.

—Oh, come on – I only want a bit of nookie—.

Warren adopts his charming boyish expression, the one that usually makes Tricia melt into his arms. She's not looking at him. He makes a grab for her bum and she turns around and kicks him hard in the leg.

—Warren, I mean it. I'm going out. Why don't you go round to your crazy girlfriend Cherry's if you're so desperate? Her voice is shaking. She's struggling hard not to lose her temper in front of the man she loves.

—What? Warren is on guard. Has he said something accidentally in his sleep?

—She's unbalanced, Warren, she is not very stable.

—I've never been round to Cherry's for sex, I don't know what you're talking about.

Warren had failed his Performance and Drama option at Teacher's College.

—Beg pardon? What did you say, Warren?

—I said, I never would go to Cherry's place and just screw, you know, I mean why are we even talking about this, why would I possibly want to, you're everything to me, Tricia.

By now Warren is bright red and looking only at the floor.

Tricia is disgusted. —Warren, you look me in the eye and you tell me – tell me the truth, Warren – have you and Cherry – done it – since you've been going out with me?

—No, says Warren, weakly.

—Look at me, Warren. If it's true, I forgive you. Just tell me the truth. If you love me you won't lie to me – will you? Tricia's voice rises to a sob. She's thinking of the dentist, and the barman, and all her missed opportunities. The sound of her unhappiness is more than Warren can bear.

—Tricia, I love you so much,— he's getting choked up himself, —you are the best thing that ever happened to me—

—Oh, Warren, says Tricia, mascara running down her cheeks.

—Only a few times I swear, only once or twice, not for ages, oh, Tricia, can you ever forgive me? Please forgive me—.

He's on his knees now clutching Tricia's calves. She looks down at him. She looks up at the ceiling. She looks into her own heart.

—Warren, I don't know what to say. That girl is a very sick girl. It sickens me to think you could be with her and then be with me, it really does.

—Trish—.

—Let me finish, Warren. I just feel tainted by the whole thing. You have tainted my femininity, Warren, and that is a lot to ask me to forgive.

Tricia steps out of Warren's clasp and puts her coat on.

—Now I'm going out. This will take time, Warren, time.

She leaves Warren wiping his eyes on the floor and goes over to her friend Viki's place. They get drunk and decide to put a brick through Cherry's window. They drive around looking for her house but Tricia can't remember properly which street it's in. On their way back to Viki's they are pulled over. Viki is breathalyzed. Tricia calls Warren from the police station.

—

Cherry dials for pizza. She leaves the money in an envelope on her doorstep. When she's sure the delivery car has driven away, she opens the door just far enough to snatch the pizza inside. She takes it into her bedroom. She looks at it and smells it for a long time. She calculates how much oil they used, how greasy it is, how many calories it contains. She has never been so hungry in her entire life. The smell of it makes her light-headed. She goes into the kitchen and comes back with a large bowl. She picks up a piece of pizza and lifts it to her mouth. Time is standing still. She is salivating. She opens her mouth and puts the end of the pizza slice on her tongue. She closes her mouth around it. She bites and chews. The sensation of having food in her mouth is something she's been aching for for so long she starts to cry. The food seems the most comforting, safest thing in the world. She's frightened to acknowledge how good it tastes. She chews and chews, and just before she swallows the bite of pizza she brings the bowl up to her face and spits everything that's inside her mouth into it. She eats half the pizza in this way, chewing and then spitting out, and then she throws the other half in the rubbish. She goes to the bathroom and cleans her teeth. She can't stop spitting out. There might be a little bit of pizza she hasn't quite got. She rinses and rinses and scrubs her gums until the basin is spattered with watery red.

—

Tricia reads her book. Wonders what hers and Warren's baby would look like.

—

The phone call comes and Cherry is summoned to the Labour Department at 9 am sharp for an interview with one of the Employment Service officials. She knew her luck couldn't last. Now she's got to figure out a story for them, a legitimate reason why she hasn't tried once to get a job in the last two years. Just the thought of the Labour Department enrages her. What do they want from her? Can't they leave her alone? If they cut off her benefit she'll be fucked.

She calls Warren's place. Doesn't mind if it's him or Tricia that answers. Either one will do.

—Yo.

It's Warren. Cherry's tempted to say something filthy, or breathe heavily into the receiver. But she doesn't want to give herself away.

—Hello?

She begins to regret banning Warren from her house. Maybe it would be okay for him to start coming round again, just on a casual basis, just for a diversion.

—Cherry?

Shit. Tricia's told him.

—Tricia's going to call the cops if you don't stop this Cherry. OK? And she knows about us. So just – piss off.

He hangs up.

This isn't fair. This is worse than any obscenity he could have yelled down the phone at her. She just wants to play with them. Isn't that all right? What's she going to do now? She doesn't know anyone else to ring anymore. Does he expect her to call strangers? Fuck him. Fuck her. Fuck the lot of them. What's she going to do now?

The phone rings while Cherry's still holding it. She drops

it in fright. She can hear a recorded message reminding her about her Labour Department appointment.

When she first started going out with Warren her favourite part of the day was waiting for him to finish work and come round. Everything she did to fill in the time meant something because she was waiting.

—

She looks in the mirror. She takes her clothes off. She finds her Labour Department form and some money for the bus. She decides against body make-up. She doesn't need it any more. On her way to the bus stop she stops to unhook the bell from her gate and hangs it, on its chain, around her neck.

# a place where no one knows your face

Your fingers are crossed because you've seen a white horse and until you see a black dog you have to keep them crossed.

White horse white horse give me good luck
onetwothreefourfivesixseveneightnineten.

Sometimes you cross the fingers on both hands because this means double luck. Also it means one hand can keep crossed if the other one gets tired, or has to reach out and pinch your sister, who is sitting squashed against the car door as far away from you as she can because (she says) you stink.

This is not fair because last week at school you punched a boy who was mean to her. He wasn't mean on purpose but he threw a basketball across the quad and she was standing in the way and it hit her in the face. You saw her small and crying and you went up to him and you punched him. You also did it because he's Jeremy Lovegrove's younger brother and you like Jeremy Lovegrove but he doesn't like you. 'He doesn't even know I'm alive,' is what you sometimes say to your reflection in the mirror. It is a phrase you read in a book. 'He doesn't even know I exist.' But the truth is he does know, he just doesn't care that much, and he has brown hair and sandy limbs and you are a bit weird. Punching his brother who is younger than you is not a good way to make Jeremy Lovegrove like you. But you don't understand this collision of aggression and love, and besides it makes you feel better. You hit Jeremy Lovegrove's younger brother because you are afraid of the power Jeremy Lovegrove has over you by not liking you when you like him, and this makes you angry. You are angry with yourself and with Jeremy Lovegrove and also with his younger brother, partly because he looks like him and partly because he threw a basketball at your sister's head.

Your sister who is sitting with hair curled around her thumb and her thumb shoved in her mouth, sucking it even though she's not a baby any more. She looks at you and pushes her nose up with her finger and then looks away. You hate her. You will torture her later. She's a scaredy-cat and when you get to the camping ground it will be no sweat to catch her off her guard and give her a fright. Be a nasty monster, Dracula or Werewolf-Man. Stalk her slowly, put a pillow up the back of your jersey like a hunchback, reach your hands out for her neck with their fingers all stretched and pointy. Wolfie's here. She will scream and scream. She is frightened of you. She doesn't know how to fight against these sort of games. She doesn't even know that she could.

Your mother passes peaches back from the front seat. You uncross the fingers of your left hand so you can hold the peach. She tells you not to get juice everywhere. You don't see how you're going to be able not to. The peach is over-ripe and squashy and as soon as you bite into it juice dribbles down your chin. It will be sticky later. The squeaking of the furry peach skin gives you shivers. You bite around a bruise. You unwind the window and throw the bruise bit out. It doesn't go out properly and slides down the door of the car. You hope your father didn't see. You stick your face out the window to feel the air rushing over it. You stick your tongue out to be dried by the air and then put it to the peach flesh and feel the spit rushing back into your mouth. Saliva. You hate that word.

You are driving past pine trees. It is a forest. Wolves probably live there. The sun is bright on the road and the shadows of the pine trees sit blackly on top of the shiny tar. For a while you count the telegraph poles. Then you breathe in and out by them. In as you pass one, hold it, out as you pass the next one, then in again. It makes you breathe slower than normal and you don't like it so you stop. Your fingers are tacky and sore from being crossed. You swap the peach stone over to your right hand and cross the fingers of your left. You bring the stone up to your mouth to suck the last bit of fruit from it and it splits in your fingers and as it drops in your lap you see two earwigs crawl out. You scream. Your father slams on the brakes. You jerk forward. You squirm around in your seat trying to see where the earwigs have landed. Your father pulls the car over. He shouts at you. It isn't fair because you can't help it if there were insects inside your peach and now they're on the car floor somewhere and going to crawl up your leg. When he's finished telling you off he pulls back out onto the road. Your face is hot. You stick it out the window again. You're not going to look at your mother and you're specially not going to look at your sister. You don't have to anyway.

You're looking at the pine trees and your castle is in behind there somewhere and it's big and made of stone and you live there and do magic. You can talk without moving your lips. It's called telepathy. You and the knights at your castle can hear each other's thoughts. Only the ones you want them to. And you've got ESP and you can move objects just by looking at them. That's called telekinesis. You've got that, like right now you could make a telegraph pole fall over or make your sister's own hand fly up and slap her on the cheek. All you have to do is concentrate hard enough. The telegraph poles are no good at the moment because the car's moving past them too fast. Later when you get to the camping ground you'll do it. Make the tent fall over or something. Make the billy boil all by itself.

The pine forest ends and you're driving through a small town. You don't like this. You don't like the small town houses with their curtains pulled closed. They look like they're blind. You imagine people living behind those curtains as only being shadows moving. The flat footpaths scare you. The flat skies scare you. It's all so big and so small at the same time. You drive up to some shops. Your sister's saying Icecream icecream icecream. Your dad stops the car and gets out. Stopped in this small town. He gets out and walks up to the dairy. He pauses in the doorway to pull up his socks and then he disappears into the blackness of the

shop. Two boys are leaning, squinting, against the wall
outside. One of them has a bike. He holds onto it lightly
with just one hand resting on the handle. It's a chopper with
a flag on the back. Him and his friend havé got jeans on.
You're not allowed to wear jeans. The boys see you looking
at them and they try to stare you down. You win the staring
competition. You always do, even if it makes your eyes
water. The boy without the bike has got freckles. They're
big and blotchy on his face, like tea-leaves. You can almost
count them. Your dad comes out of the dairy holding Tip-
tops. He gets in the car and hands them out. Your mum
says, Eat it before it melts. You peel off the wrapper with
your teeth and suck the cold hard chocolate coating. The
boys are watching. You've got an icecream and they haven't.
You bite into it, closing your eyes and going mmm like in
the ads as the chocolate cracks in your mouth and you taste
the creamy middle bit. You curl your lips up and smile your
mean smile at them, waving the icecream back and forth
and moving your head from side to side. Your dad starts the
car. The boys give you the fingers. You can't do them back
because you've got one hand full of icecream and stick and
one hand with the fingers glued together with peach juice.
All you can do is poke out your tongue in the back
windscreen while they wave their arms up and down,
straight out in front of them, fingers held up in Vs. Fuck shit
bugger damn you say in your head. Then you say, Sorry God
please God I'll never say it or think it again God, never ever
as long as I live, sorry God sorry.

You twist back in your seat to face front again. And your

bloody shit damn sister's eating her icecream slowly, tiny baby bites so she'll have heaps left when you're finished and she can gloat about it. You don't really care because you feel sick anyway, icecream and peach and marmite and lettuce sandwich and a hard-boiled egg all churning round inside. The heat outside. The road, starting to wind now over a hill. You think you might chuck. You tell your mum you have a headache. She goes Tch and sighs. Close your eyes she says. You do and it makes the swinging of the car worse. Rolling back and forward, swinging, going up and down over dips and little bumpy bits. Mum, you say, Mum. She turns and looks at you. She's green, says your sister. She's all green. Your mum reaches her hand back and squeezes your knee. You'll be all right, she says. Not long now. How long, how lo-ong says your sister. Shhh says your mum, looking in the glove box for something. She hands you a barley sugar. Suck this.

Dad, says your sister, Dad, do A for horses. He doesn't hear her. Your mother nudges him. She murmurs something. He glances quickly round at you and your sister. He smiles. A for 'orses, he says slowly, B for mutton—. You join in. C for yourself, D for dumb. You know this game. Your dad knows it from when he was a little boy. Most of the things in it are from the olden days. From that time when your dad was running round in shorts and playing marbles and the war was on. The marbles are still at your Gran's place. G for police. I for Novello. L for leather. That's a good one, getting to hear your Dad say 'hell' even though he's not really saying it. O for the wings of a dove. You look up in the sky and see a hawk circling. They swoop down and eat the eyes out of baby lambs. At your castle you keep them tame and they carry messages for you. Z for breezes, your dad says, and your sister says Again again. But your mum starts singing her favourite car song, in her low and whispery voice. I know – a dark – secluded place – a place – where no one knows your face – a glass – of wine – a fast embrace – it's called – Hernando's Hideaway. You imagine the room, lit with low yellow light and filled with Spanish music. Ladies like on the back of your playing cards, with big spotty dresses on, frills and flowers in their hair. Just knock – three times – and whisper low – that you – and I – were sent by Joe. You will be free – to gaze at me and talk – of – lo-ove. Your mum goes to that place. Well, she did before you were born maybe. She spent nights in Hernando's Hideaway, smoking cigarettes with a man in a hat and dancing to castanets. Your mother sings, looking every now and then at her own reflection in the window. There's a funny twist to her mouth when the song is over.

I want a barley sugar says your sister, I want one too. Grow up, you say. Yours is gone and you don't feel sick any more. You glare at her. Your mum passes a barley sugar over to her. See, I got one, she says to you. Grow up, you say again. She pretends she can't hear you. The car goes over a really big bump. Your sister yelps. I swallowed mine, Mum, I swallowed mine. Shhh, says your mother. You mimic your sister under your breath. You make your voice whiny and high. I thwallowed mine. Shut up, she says. Thut up, you say. Stop it, she says. Thtop it. Mum, she says. Mu-um.

Make her stop. Make her thtop. Shut your face. Thut your fathe. You can see your mother in the front with her sunglasses on and her eyes shut, humming. Your dad is frowning at the road. Your sister pinches your leg. You slap her hand. Ow, she says. Ow, you echo. She tries to dead-arm you. You rap her knee with your knuckles. She scratches your hand. You grab her wrist and say, Want a chinese burn? She tries to pull away but you are stronger than her. Do you? No. Say please. No. Say please most beautiful sister. You start to twist the skin a little bit. She looks as if she might start bawling. You don't like the way you feel. You feel like a big fat giant. You throw her wrist back into her lap. Crybaby, you say, turning to the window again. She sits and rubs her wrist for a minute. Then she leans over and pinches your arm really hard. You let her do it. If you two don't stop you can get out here, says your dad. You roll your eyes. Dick, you whisper. You glance at your sister. He's a dick, you whisper to her. She giggles. You rub your arm. He eats turds for breakfast, you say. Big fat smelly ones. She giggles again. You say, What's red and gets smaller and smaller and smaller? What? she says. A baby combing its hair with a potato peeler, you say. She laughs even though you can tell she doesn't really get it. Hey, Mum and Dad, listen to this. What's red and gets smaller and smaller and smaller? What, dear? says your mother. A baby combing its hair with a potato peeler. You and your sister force big laughs out, ha ha ha. Oh, that's dreadful, says your mother. Really.

It's so hot in the car. Even with the window open it's

boiling. You're driving past dry brown paddocks. Cows look at you when you go past. Sheep don't. You wonder if black sheep know they're different. Sheep look nice from far off but when you get up close they smell of dags and things. Their wool looks soft but it's not really. It's greasy and thick. You drive past a sign that says One Way Jesus. Dumb. That doesn't even make sense. You feel sleepy. There's nowhere comfortable to put your head. You curl up as little as you can and close your eyes, listen to the car engine, the wheels on the road.

When you wake up your legs have got pins and needles. You were dribbling, says your sister. Was not, you say, wiping the wet seat, grumpy from sleep. So thirsty. The countryside smells. Silage is what it's called. And there's bits of paddocks covered with black plastic that's held down by old tyres. You wish you could read your book in the car without feeling sick. In your book the countryside is full of robins and pussywillow and little stone cottages. Ramshackle. There's a twinkly old farmer, and winding lanes and streams and primroses. The car bounces again and your stomach lurches. The road's bumpy and dusty, loose shingle. You must be getting closer to the camping ground. There's that funny red clay you never see anywhere else. In your book the kids have boarding school and tuck boxes. They eat sandwiches with the crusts cut off them. Pony club and gymkhanas. At the camping ground last year, they had a horse race along the beach on New Year's Day. You imagine winning it this year, the kids' race, miles ahead of everyone on your beautiful white horse that lives at the castle. And at the end of the race everyone just about falls over because you say the magic words to your horse and it starts to fly. It's got wings and you can fly as far as you like, high above the beach, over the bush and the hills and into another world where there are stone cottages and pussywillow and winding magic lanes.

You close your eyes again. Somewhere out of your dreams the car stops. Are we there? you say, stretching your neck. It's cooler now and the sun's not so bright. Soon, says your mum. Dad's getting fish and chips. Can I have L&P? you say. Go in and ask him. You open the door and almost fall out. Your feet feel strange on the ground. Put your jandals on, says your mother. You slip them on and stand swaying a bit outside the car. Your legs are all wobbly. You see your dad in the fish and chip shop. It's bright inside and you blink. You ask your dad if you can have L&P. He says yes. You lean against his leg. He puts his arm round your shoulder. The fish and chip shop smells of hot fat and sausages. You look out the glass door to the car. Your mother's leaning against it smoking a cigarette and looking down the road. Your sister's got her feet up on the seat and her knees up to her chin, sucking her thumb. You feel grown up. There's a purple electric light along the back wall. What's that dad? It's for killing flies, he says. They fly into it and get electrocuted. That's dreadful, you say. Really. The fish and chip shop man hands you a potato fritter in a white paper bag with see-through spots of grease on it. The fat fish and chip shop lady comes in through the plastic curtain strips that hang in the doorway to the other room. Long drive? she asks your father. We came from Wellington, he says, and she nods, waves fat fingers at you. The man shakes salt on everything and wraps it in newspaper and gives it to your dad.

The four of you sit in the car as it's getting dark eating your fish and chips. There's flies in there, you tell your sister, pointing to her chips. Are not, she says. Your fingers are salty. The car smells of food. You let your sister have a drink of your L&P. We'll be pitching the tent in the dark again, your mum says to your dad. Don't worry, you say, I can put it up by myself. You'll do telepathy on it and it will all go in the right place. You look out the window at the dirty street and think of your big stone castle. Even though you're sitting in the car with your mum and dad and your sister you feel as if you're all alone.

You take everyone's chip paper to the rubbish bin across the road. A black dog runs past. You forgot.

# after mcdonald's

Marcelle and Diana know each other from when they both worked at McDonald's one summer. It was the break after their big exams at school. They bonded over their mutual fury at having to wear green Crimplene slacks and 'fucking stupid' hats. They both resented the clock punching and till balancing, the crap pay and smell of grease. They made this known. They were not popular with management. Diana would mock the ambitions of the other staff, spotty kids to whom it was crucial that they be awarded the golden prize of a Happy Team Member of the Month photograph beside the fries warmer. Marcelle performed cruel imitations of the Team Leader, a relentlessly efficient Christian boy with two kids already and a Scouting background. Jesus Christ, both Diana and Marcelle would say loudly when he was nearby. Bloody *hell*. God: a perfect teenage sneer. Marcelle's imitations were brilliant. She was going to be an actress. And Diana was going to be a poet.

They left McDonald's under a cloud. Neither of them had achieved Happy status over the three months of summer

and neither were invited to stay on in a part-time capacity
after school. They didn't give a fuck. What could it matter
when there was a whole world out there to explore – their
careers as artists!

Together, they made a lot of plans for a one-woman-
show. Diana would write it for Marcelle to star in. This was
the way, they decided, that you got things done. Collabora-
tion between two creative people. The play would be unique
– fresh, funny, up-to-the-minute. It would be about the lives
of people just like them, young women searching for something – on the brink of something important. But it wouldn't
be only a woman thing. That was essential. They were sure
that once Diana had it written they would find a director
and a venue. Maybe they could make a short film of it as
well. Once it was written, that was the thing.

After McDonald's, Marcelle declared her refusal to work
in the service industry ever again. Though it was Diana who
had been the more scathing about the place, Marcelle had
been deeply offended by the idea of having to be nice to
people she didn't like, and especially those who could do
nothing for her. When she started the drama classes and
audition rounds, she found that being nice was something
that came naturally as a practical necessity. She didn't like
to call it 'networking', but she did understand the import-
ance of being seen at opening nights, workshops and screen-
tests for breath freshener commercials. It also helped her
avoid service work that her sister owned a house with a
spare room where Marcelle could live rent-free.

Diana moved from one café job to another, moaning all

the time about the customers and the other staff and the chefs who were invariably wankers. Every now and then she would determine to quit a job and 'write full-time', but within a month she'd find herself walking into places and asking whether they were hiring. It wasn't just the money.

Meanwhile, Marcelle met with some success on the fringes of the alternative theatre scene. There were a few non-speaking roles in the *It's New So Fuck You* one-act play festival, which she doubled with her job as stage manager. She appeared naked (except for mud) on stage in an adaptation of *Wuthering Heights*, playing An Elemental Force. She wore a bikini in an outdoor production of *The Bacchae*. This was in winter, and Marcelle got her first mention in a mainstream paper: 'notable', it said, 'for the unique shade of blue which coloured her legs and arms; a very pretty blue, the like of which this reviewer had not seen before.' She is now rehearsing the role of Varia in *The Cherry Orchard* for Callum O'Donnell's company, which is something of a coup – or a sell-out, depending on which way you look at it.

What would you call yourself, they used to ask each other. Actor or actress? Writer or author or poet? Lady author? Poetess? This was a serious topic and one worth giving considerable thought. Not only was there the matter of your CV – they were at the forefront of the gender battle here and certain issues had to be cleared up. No diminutives, please. Unless, of course, it was going to impede career progress to make a big fuss about it.

For Marcelle, it usually depends on who she's telling. In The Cherry Orchard Company she is definitely an 'actress'. Most of her fringe theatre friends are 'actors', 'workers', or 'performance radicals'. Who cares, Diana decides eventually. Waiter, waitress – it's all the same to her.

Diana is putting the finishing touches to what she hopes will be her first published collection of poetry. She has sent many single poems off before, to literary magazines and journals. So far she has not had anything accepted. This is depressing, but she has high expectations for the *Collected Poems*. She thinks they will benefit from being read all together – this way her themes will be more apparent. Recently she has been experimenting with haiku, which she enjoys because she can write ten in one morning. She writes haiku of her dreams; haiku about flowers; haiku about death. Death is what she writes about most, listening to The Cure, REM and Joy Division. 'This Is Not a Love Song' is her favourite. She prides herself on not writing anything – not haiku, sonnets, or anything – about love. Love sucks.

Death preoccupies Diana while she's working the espresso machine. She froths milk and wipes out coffee grounds and contemplates mortality. Death, she decides, must be like white space. That's what all those near-death-experience people say – a tunnel, a light, a voice, and beyond that – white space. White space, like a window. A sheet on a washing line. A blank page. Hang on! There's something in this: a blank page = white space = death. Amazing. It's almost a haiku. And if a blank page equals death, then by writing – by writing she is defeating death. Creating life! This is fantastic. She can't wait to finish work so she can tell Marcelle.

—What I don't understand, says Marcelle to the room in general, —is, if Varia's so desperate for Lopakhin to ask her to marry him, why doesn't she just say so?

There is a silence. The actor playing Lopakhin sighs and sits down on the floor. The stage manager unsurreptitiously looks at her stopwatch.

—I mean, is that stupid?

The director pinches the bridge of his nose. He smiles with his mouth and nods once, as if at an inevitability. Sucks his teeth.

—No, he says. —It's a very good question. Now, shall we try the scene again?

Diana photocopies the poems – a nice round one hundred in all – on to A5 paper. She buys cardboard and staples the paper into it so it resembles a book. She stencils the working title on the front: *Living in the Margins*. It looks good, professional. Real. Her first baby! She is full of hope for it. Yes, she's nervous, but also quietly confident. She wraps it up lovingly and with care. The covering letter takes longer to write than most of the poems – how to present herself, how to say enough to make them interested without saying too much – well, in the end, she feels, the work will speak for itself. She kisses the parcel and she sends it off. And then she waits.

What would she do, Marcelle used to ask Diana, when she won some big literary prize? What would she do with the money? Donate it to charity? Buy a house? Stop waitressing? They'd also talk about how Marcelle would deal with recognition in public; how hard it would be to combine family with an acting career; the problem of ageing.

It was fantastic how supportive of each other they were. There was no silly competitiveness, no rivalry. Leave that sort of thing to the boys. It was one of the brilliant things about being women – they shared what was important and looked out for each other. They didn't want to fall into any 'earth mother' stereotypes, but – it had to be said – they were nurturers. And at the end of the day they valued the friendship far above any careerist bullshit.

For example, Diana always attends Marcelle's opening nights. It's an act of loyalty – truth is she's never been a huge fan of theatre – but she makes the effort for friendship's sake. It seems to her that Marcelle must be talented – she's certainly difficult not to notice on stage. What exactly draws you to her is hard to pinpoint. A way she has of moving around all the time perhaps, or of sighing loudly. This, Diana supposes, must be 'stage presence'. She's sure Marcelle will be a success, but she herself finds the whole theatre scene both intimidating and dull. She has not confessed this to Marcelle, who still refers often to their plans for a one-woman show. It's not that Diana's opposed to the idea of them working on something together – but perhaps a better project would be a reading/performance of Diana's haiku and other writings. It would be possible on a tiny budget – they could tour, maybe put out an audio tape. Imagine how wide an audience she could introduce to her work! Even if she doesn't hear back from that publisher, nothing will stop her from finding her public. She's no quitter. Yeah, that's another great thing about women – their stamina.

—Thank you, says Marcelle, smiling, her face luminous. —Thank you all so much.

She lowers her eyes for a minute, collects herself and smiles out again.

—I've been lucky. I've had some wonderful teachers. I want to acknowledge their great skill— pause, laugh, —and great patience— she waits for the audience to finish laughing, —and most of all I want to thank them for their faith in me. All of us know what it's like to struggle.

She's trying to keep the emotion out of her voice. Clutches the shampoo bottle tighter.

—My most heartfelt thanks must go to my husband, Callum O'Donnell. Without you— she looks hard, to single him out of the dark crowd, —without you, I would not be here today.

Damn, the mirror's misting up. She rubs it clear with her fist. Still looking good.

—And nor would our beautiful twins, Jack and Ella.

She lets her joy shine through, lighting up the room. Holds the shampoo bottle high in a gesture expressing triumph, gratitude and humility all at once.

—Marcelle! Her sister pounds on the bathroom door.
—Are you ever coming out of there? I'm late for work.

Diana doesn't want to make a big deal about it, but you'd
think that some places could get back to you a bit faster
when you've sent them your writing. It's only polite.

Before Marcelle got her first speaking part (it was a wailing
part really, in *Wuthering Heights*), she and Diana would
meet regularly at the gym to work off their creative frustra-
tions in step class. The bit Marcelle looked forward to
most was the sauna afterwards and herbal tea in the cafe-
teria, but as time went on it became harder and harder to
drag Diana away from the aerobics room. She would stay on
for a second class and then do twenty minutes on the
weights circuit. She started to talk about taking up kick
boxing.

Marcelle worried a bit about what all Diana's exercising
might be for. 'Mental health' was the reason Diana gave, but
her obsession with it struck Marcelle as anything but healthy.
She herself never managed to experience an endorphin rush
after a cardiofunk class. She felt this as a small failure on her
part.

Once Marcelle was in rehearsals for *Wuthering*, she fell
out of the habit of going to the gym. There were so many
other things to do – read the book, see the movie, spend
long hours discussing The Gothic with the rest of the cast.
Diana, however, kept up and even increased her attendance.
Instead of rising early to write, as she used to, she would jog

to the gym and get in a couple of circuits before going to the restaurant. Her legs were like rock. Her stomach was unbelievably flat. When the first rejection slip came through from a national magazine, she went out and bought herself some useful little rubber anklebands.

She rolls cutlery in prep for lunch while doing her leg exercises. The rubber band is around her ankles. She sits there scissoring her legs, feeling her hips shrink by the minute. The timer on the oven goes off. Eleven o'clock. She stands up and geisha-walks to the telephone. Her flatmate Troy answers.

—Hello?

—It's me. Is it there yet?

—I'll just look.

Diana does some quick knee-bends while she waits.

—Uh, there's a bill . . . and a postcard for me – hey, it's from Lulu, cool – and, yeah, a letter for you.

—Open it, open it.

—It looks personal – Dear Di, It's been very hot here this past week—

—Oh, shit. It's just my mother. OK, forget it.

—Sorry, Di. I'll call if anything else comes. Late delivery maybe?

—Yeah, sure.

Diana shuffles back to the knives and forks. Damn it to hell. She's going to have to wait at least another entire day.

There were, despite the closeness of their friendship, subjects that Marcelle and Diana did not discuss. These taboos were of Diana's making – Marcelle was uninhibited by nature and simply avoided the topics in deference to Diana's squeamishness, which was not unlike the squeamishness of a seven-year-old boy. Any 'body stuff' or 'romantic stuff' was completely out of bounds. Marcelle had once confessed to a crush on an actor she knew, and Diana's reaction had been unexpectedly hostile. Boring, she'd said. Don't want to talk about that bullshit. Jesus, Marcelle, there's more important things in life. Death, for instance. Ever think about death?

Marcelle didn't, but nor did she mind Diana's response too badly – she did have other friends with whom she could talk freely about sex. And it meant there was something more worthwhile about her conversations with Diana, something more valuable. She felt very virtuous about the fact they spent so much time together discussing their careers.

—Of course, says Diana, —it's easy for you. You *have* a career.

They are out for dinner. The food is a long time coming.

They're on to their second bottle of wine.

—So do you, says Marcelle. It's not strictly true, but she feels as if she should say something reassuring.

—No, I don't. What, waitressing? Yeah, I really think so.

—You're a writer.

—Unpublished.

—Yeah, but you do it, you know. I really envy you that. If you want to write, you can just do it – wherever you are, whenever you need to express yourself. But if I want to act, say, if I have a need to express *myself* through *my* art, I have to wait for somebody else to employ me. You know?

—Yes, says Diana, —you're right. It's much, much easier for me. I can't believe how easy I've got it. I'm so lucky! Any time of the day or night, if inspiration strikes – bam – I just drop whatever I'm doing – carrying five plates to a table of suits, maybe – and pop off to a corner and jot it down. Luxury.

—Yeah, okay. It's not that simple. But writing is a much more portable profession. All you need is a pencil and paper.

—Marcelle, I'm really not in the mood, says Diana. —I'm sorry. I just can't spend another night having another fantasy conversation about how perfect my life's going to be when I'm in a little converted barn in Spain banging away on a portable typewriter and coming up with the great twenty-first-century novel. It's bullshit. There won't even be a twenty-first-century novel. And I'll never get out of this goddamn country. Fuck it.

Marcelle studies her fingernails. Oh boy. Poor Diana, she's having a real crisis. It's so hard to feel validated when no one appreciates your work. She is overcome with guilt for having had a lucky break. But she'll never leave Diana behind. When her career takes off, she'll get a commission for Diana to write her a screenplay. Something to showcase her talents – a stunning cinematic début, they will say – shines brighter than any other actress of her generation – fresh, funny, up-to-the-minute. Yeah. Reminiscent of the young Ingrid Bergman . . . the new Garbo . . . utterly captivating . . . the beginning of an important career. Marcelle smiles, and digs her fingernails into her palms with excitement.

—It's going to be fine, she tells Diana. —We'll sort it all out.

—Yeah, right, says Diana, waving their empty wine bottle at the waitress. —Whatever.

The eleven o'clock phone call ritual is beginning to get Diana down. She has heard that if they do want to publish you, they get back to you straight away. No mucking around. So what could this delay be for?

Marcelle waits for Diana in a bar after rehearsal. She looks over her notes. In love with Lopakhin, she reads. Why headscarf? Walk??? She had hoped it wouldn't be another unglamorous role. This might be her first foray into trad theatre – Chekhov, she could hardly believe it – but it looked as if she wouldn't yet be escaping dowdy costumes, or enjoying hours at the dressing-room mirror.

A girl she knows from kabuki classes at the community centre glances over but then walks past as if she hasn't seen her.

Marcelle calls out. The girl turns and fakes surprise.

—Oh, hi, Marcelle.

—Hi. How are you?

—Fine. I hear you're doing *The Cherry Orchard*.

—Yeah. It's really exciting.

—So, six months of sucking up to Callum O'Donnell at opening nights has paid off then?

Marcelle smiles nervously. Is that a joke?

—See ya, says the girl, and walks away, flicking her hair over her shoulders with both hands.

Marcelle is stunned. How rude can you get? That girl must be really threatened. Well, if they're jealous, what can she do? An actor, she tells herself, has to be oblivious to pettiness and envy. She is concerned with higher things. She must concentrate on her work. It's not as if she ever 'sucked up' to Callum anyway. They have a natural affinity. A mutual admiration of each other's integrity. And – yes, she has to admit it, it's important that she's truly honest with herself – they share a sexual attraction for each other. Not that that's why she got the part, but if things develop outside of rehearsals – then, why deny it?

Eleven o'clock rolls around again. Diana makes the call.

—Troy? Me.

—It's not here yet. Call back.

She calls back at eleven-ten, then at eleven twenty-five.

—What do you suppose is the matter?

—He's just late today, that's all. Look I'll call you.

But Troy doesn't call, and Troy doesn't call. The lunch rush starts. Diana can't concentrate. She needs to know. Gets someone to cover her tables and sneaks the mobile phone into the staff loos. Troy's not home. The answer phone's on.

Shit, she thinks, what if it's there? What if it comes today? The suspense is killing her.

She tells the manager she's sick. Has to go home. Really

sorry. The manager, overbooked and prematurely grey from stress, says, If you have to leave now don't bother coming back. Diana says, Fuck you then. Mutters as she is walking out the door, Fat bitch, why don't you get your jaw wired?

—You'll never work in the food industry again, the manager calls after her. I heard that!

Diana waves a taxi down and sits on the edge of the seat all the way home. She bursts in the door and searches the hall for any mail. Maybe it's in the kitchen. No. Maybe Troy put it in her bedroom. No. She goes upstairs and rings the bell.

—Excuse me, I'm wondering if there might have been any mail delivered here for me by accident?

No.

She stops and thinks about things. She's just lost her job. Oh great. How fucking great her life is turning out to be. What a really wonderful time she's having. How totally, totally cool.

Leo, the guy playing Lopakhin, asks Marcelle if she wants to have lunch with him. They get a sandwich and sit in the park.

—Don't you just love watching people wandering by? Marcelle asks. —I love inventing different lives for them. And the different ways they move! The human body is a really amazing thing, you know?

—Yeah, says Leo finally.

—So, how do you think rehearsals are going?

A bit of tomato falls out of her sandwich and on to her

leg. She brushes it off and rubs at the stain. Is he deaf or something?

—They're fine, says Leo, his mouth full.

—Callum's really great, isn't he?

—He's OK. Leo licks his fingers. —He's a lousy lay though.

—Oh. Are you, um – having an, um—

—Oh, nah, says Leo, —Off and on. Listen Michelle—

—Marcelle, she mumbles.

—Sorry, yeah. Marcelle, I think there's a problem with the chemistry between Varia and Lopakhin. It doesn't really click, right?

—Oh.

—You know, I don't feel as if I'm getting enough from you. I know it's your first big job, but we're three weeks into it now, you know? I mean, are you holding back for a reason?

He waits. Marcelle shakes her head, slowly.

—Yeah, well. Give it some thought, OK? I've got to get back. Oh, yeah – I think Callum wants a word with you after rehearsal tonight. See you in there.

She watches as he gets to his feet and stretches, eyes behind their shades roving lazily around the park. He saunters off on his stupid long legs.

Marcelle rolls over on to her stomach and hugs the earth, as her yoga teacher has taught her to do when she is feeling unloved.

Diana turns REM up as loud as they will go. She wants to scream! She's so frustrated! She feels like doing something really dramatic, something really violent. She yanks open her desk drawer. A cup of cold coffee on the desk falls over with the movement. She sweeps her arm across the desk and knocks everything on it onto the floor, coffee cup included. Getting into it now, she pulls the whole drawer out and smashes it several times on the edge of the desk. A splinter flies up and hits her in the eye. She runs through the house shouting, Fuck. Fuck. Forces her eye open in the bathroom mirror. Gets the splinter out, tears running down one side of her face.

Fuck, she yells again. Sits on the corner of the bath. Kicks her heels against it. Shit. Hell.

But somewhere, in the midst of all the redness and fury, a part of her still believes that she's going to get it. That the letter saying Yes is going to arrive. It might not be today. It might not be tomorrow. But she will get it. She must, because she's earned it. Nobody should have to put up with this shit without some kind of reward at the end. It's got to be a matter of time. There's no way that luck can smile on someone like Marcelle and not on her.


—Can you smell anything? Grace, the girl playing Anya, leans over towards Marcelle and sniffs.

Marcelle frowns. —I don't think so. Like what?

Grace sniffs again, and pouts her pretty mouth. —Like something gross. A dead thing or something.

—Can I have everyone's attention please, says Callum before Marcelle can reply. —I want to try a run of Act Two this afternoon. Let's have a quick, focusing warm-up. Freeze-tag. Marcelle, you're It.

# after mcdonald's

The others scatter around the rehearsal room. Marcelle lunges after them, getting breathless fast amidst shrieks of laughter and squeals. She's too slow, her feet aren't agile enough, her arms are too short. She gets Gayev in a corner but he dodges out before she can tag him. Now everyone's grouped up at the other end of the hall and she's lumbering towards them. She wants Callum to stop the game. Is hot, panting, sticky. Smells something sweet and awful, like dogshit.

—Come on, Marcelle, shouts Callum. —Attack, attack! Focus!

She takes a deep breath and charges the group. They peel off inevitably and gracefully until she is facing the blank wall. She turns sharply, sees Pischik out of the corner of her eye, reaches out for him – is he slowing down on purpose, out of pity? – and goes over on her ankle, twisting it underneath her as she crashes to the floor.

Actors surround her, pick her up, pat her shoulders – are you okay? Jesus, that was a hard fall – laughing to show her that it's not so bad, to cover up the embarrassment. She laughs too, to show them it's not so bad, she's resilient, fine, really, no, it's fine. Drags herself over to a chair and rubs her ankle, smiling brightly, knowing she'll die if the tears in her eyes spill over on to her cheeks. Pulls her jumper off – needs to cool down – and the dogshit smell rises up again stronger than before. Realizes that the mud she'd brushed off her T-shirt after hugging the ground in the park was not in fact mud at all.

—Excuse me a minute.

She limps to the bathroom, takes her T-shirt off and shoves it in the bin, packing paper towels down on top of it so nobody sees. Puts her jumper back on. Walks back into the rehearsal room and tries to ignore the hush.

Once, during the one-act play festival, Marcelle had broken down and called Diana in tears. It was too hard, she was too tired, stage managing was too demanding, performing too terrifying. She had sat on the stairs of her house after the show one night and gulped through her sobs that she was sick of it, had had enough, was going to quit. And Diana had lain curled up on the couch in her flat saying, No, it's all right, you're so talented, you'll be fine. Marcelle had sniffed and said, Do you really think so? To which Diana had just laughed. Of course she did. She believed in Marcelle. They believed in each other. She wrote a poem about it that night and took it over in the morning. They drank tea and put their arms around each other and said, Yes, it was hard but they were going to be OK, weren't they. They were smart. They were creative. Nobody said it would be a bed of roses. But they had their belief, and they had each other. They were lucky!

Diana tells Troy that she's quit her job and she's going to write full-time. No way she's going to be a career waitress like that bitch manager at work. She goes to the gym. She goes for a run. She cleans the windows at the flat on the inside and on the outside. She sweeps the kitchen floor and polishes it. She rings up the bitch manager and apologizes.

They arrange for her to start again the next day, washing dishes. She says, OK. She says, thanks.

—I'm thinking of dyeing my hair, says Marcelle.
  —Why?
  —Oh, I think Varia might have red hair.
  —Oh.
  —There's a budget, you know, for makeup and haircuts and stuff.
  —Great.
  —My costume's pretty doggy. Varia's supposed to wear a headscarf but I don't think it's integral to the part. I think red hair will look really Russian, you know.
  —Yeah.
  —Are you coming to opening night? I've booked you a seat. You can have my comp.
  —OK.
  —Are you all right?
  —Oh, yeah, I'm fine.

Troy has brought home a copy of the very magazine that first rejected Diana. It is reminding her just how long it is that she's been sending work off and having it returned. She's tempted to chuck it straight in the bin but curiosity overcomes her. She sits down with her ankleband on and flicks through the pages. Her eye is caught by a large red headline. Young Writers Making Huge Advances: The New Poets. Underneath is a full-page piece on four – no, five – poets who have recently signed with major publishing houses. She reads through the article and does some quick maths. They are all around the same age as her. Jesus. She's not coming out on top. She's not coming out at all. Still no reply to her manuscript. For God's sake. Why doesn't she just give up?

It is after rehearsal on a wet Tuesday. Marcelle decides to walk home through the drizzle, to give herself some space to think about the play. She doesn't bother to change out of her tights and leotard top. People probably think I'm a dancer, she tells herself, back ramrod straight and feet splayed outwards. How does Varia walk? She must have something special that makes her gait unique. Marcelle has still not found the character's physical centre. She is certain it must be different from her own and she will have to explore an entirely new and challenging physicality. Today she'd tried playing her stooped over, the symbolic weight of the play pressing on her shoulders. Callum asked if there was something wrong with her back. She said no. Then why the fuck are you standing around like a crone? he shouted. You're a young woman! So that had obviously been the wrong path to take. But there must be something to deform Varia – otherwise why would Lopakhin let her go? – a limp perhaps, or a club foot. She stiffens her left leg and lurches along for a bit, practising the feel of it. She can see looks of sympathy in the eyes of people walking past. So tragic, they murmur to themselves, in one so young . . . She longs for the chance to play Laura in *The Glass Menagerie*.

Rounding a corner, she sees a familiar figure coming in

her direction on the other side of the road. It's Andrew who was in the production of *The Bacchae* with her. It doesn't look as if he's seen her yet. She swings her bag over her shoulder and breaks into the specially choreographed dance that she performed in the play. Excellent! She waves her arms to get his attention while writhing sinuously up the street towards him. The steps are all coming back to her now. High kick, arch the back, head roll and jump. Grapevine, spin, knee-dip, hop. Has he noticed her? It's hard to see any signs of recognition. She gets closer, repeating the sequence. As she prepares for another hip rotation it becomes blisteringly clear that the man is not Andrew. This guy, of average height, with the same colouring and wearing a jacket exactly like one owned by Andrew, is a total stranger. A total stranger who is looking at her in unfeigned horror. She catches his eye and he quickly looks away, staring grimly ahead. Without pausing to think Marcelle continues the dance, looks both ways for traffic, crosses the road and swerves down an empty side street. She stops abruptly, rubbing her arms and legs as if to get the recent movement out of them. Shakes her feet. Shudders. Pulls herself together and marches purposefully back to the main road to continue the journey home.

I must remember the look on that guy's face, she thinks, for when I next have to play confusion on stage.

Diana walks past McDonald's. She turns and goes back and stands outside it, looking in through the large double-glazed windows. For a minute she thinks she can see their old Team

Leader, that little slime bucket, telling some girl to wipe down a bench. But it can't be him. He'll be behind a desk somewhere now, pictures of his Happy wife and Happy children lined up all in a row. Everybody working in there today looks about fifteen or sixteen, like she and Marcelle used to be. Same unflattering uniforms, same belittling hats. A bolshy-faced boy comes and clears the table closest to the window. He takes his hat off and scratches his head. Better not let the boss catch you doing that, thinks Diana. What are hair and fingernails, everybody? The favourite hiding places of germs! And what are germs, everybody? The enemy! He notices Diana staring at him. He scowls at her. What are you staring at? he mouths. Diana shrugs and walks away. She's going to the Post Office to complain about their mail delivery, which doesn't seem to be as regular as it should.

Marcelle makes Diana come shopping with her for a dress to wear on opening night. They traipse up and down the streets trying to find the right thing.

—It would be easier, says Marcelle, —if I hadn't put all this weight on for the part.

—Have you? Diana looks her up and down. Seems like the same old slightly pear-shaped Marcelle to her.

—Oh yeah, I decided Varia's probably quite heavy. Those solid babushkas, you know. I've been taking dietary supplements.

Diana holds a skintight silver slip up for inspection, then puts it back on the rack. Marcelle sighs.

## after mcdonald's

—I hate those actors who won't look ugly for a part, don't you? I mean, if you're in it for the glamour, forget it!

—I might try this on, murmurs Diana. —Just a minute.

It's time! Marcelle is in the theatre at two o'clock in the afternoon for her warm-up. She stretches, sings, runs through her lines and checks her props. Then she does it all over again. She leaves little cards on everyone's dressing tables: Dear Uncle Gayev (ha ha), you're such a sweetie. Break a leg! Dear Grace, Your Anya is quite lovely – and don't worry at all about the wig, it looks totally natural.

Dear Leo – but she stops. Perhaps it will increase the opening night tension if she doesn't leave Leo a card. Inject a real buzz, some uncertainty. Yes, that's it. Unpredictability – that's what tonight needs. Inspiration!

Diana is at the kitchen table biting her thumbnails.

The letter came today. Troy had called the restaurant, his voice wobbling with excitement. Diana did pelvic floor exercises all through the lunch shift, cleaned every surface of that fucking kitchen until it shone, and caught the bus calmly, reasonably home. She turned the key in the door slowly and carefully. She looked at the hall floor, which was bare. She made her way to the kitchen and saw the letter there on the table. She poured herself a glass of water. She drank it, looking at the envelope with its familiar logo in the top left corner.

Suddenly she couldn't do it on her own. She needed Marcelle to be there, even just on the end of the phone, while she opened it. She called her house and got the machine. Where the hell was she? Damn, this was too scary.

With shaking fingers, she peeled the top flap of the envelope away. She lifted the paper out and put it on the table. She wiped her hands on her skirt. She unfolded the paper thinking, only the date. I'm just going to look at the date at the top. But before she could read that, before she could even see it, a word rose off the page and filled the space in front of her eyes.

Regret.

She looks up from the letter and focuses on a water stain above the sink. She puts her thumb to her mouth. She feels distracted. Isn't there something she's supposed to be doing tonight?

Marcelle throws everything into the first-night performance. Each moment she's on stage she can feel her nerveends tingling, her skin electric. She emotes as she's never emoted before. Almost faints with anxiety in Act One. Nearly loses her voice crying out for Anya in Act Two – in a flash of spontaneity she ends the act with a scream from offstage. Act Three almost breaks her heart, and Act Four – Act Four! She can barely get her lines out in the nonproposal scene with Lopakhin. Clenches her fists till she feels the skin on her palms break under her nails. When Lopakhin leaves she throws herself to the floor and weeps, loudly, for five minutes. She cannot stop – the force of Chekhov has taken over – Ranyevskaya and Anya must project their lines over her howling. She's not even aware of the audience, or the other people moving about the stage – she *is* Varia.

Sweat-drenched in the curtain call, she smiles through her tears and hears the word 'magnetic' in her head. Magnetic, chilling performance. Unstoppable. Riveting. Utterly captivating. Never before ... this seasoned reviewer ... Duse ... Bernhardt ... Knipper ...

She bows low and, rising, lifts the hands of the two actors either side of her in victory. They slip out of her grip and she sees they are clapping the audience, their heads bent as if in worship. Yes, yes, of course. She, too, applauds her – can she say it? – her peers, her colleagues, her fans.

Troy comes home and finds Diana still at the kitchen table, the room dark.

—Come on, he says, grabbing their coats from the hall. —I'll take you to the movies.

Marcelle changes into the new smock dress and brushes her shiny copper curls. She must look for Callum. But first – she heads out to the busy foyer, scanning the crowd for that familiar face – first she has to find Diana. Friend. Support. Fellow artist. Diana? Where is she? Where is she?

# let's go

Let's go to Roxy, we say. Let's go to FX.

I try to learn some of the language, but don't get beyond 'diky', which means thanks. Informal. Casual. Friendly. The formal way is 'dekuji vam', but it's easier not to bother with the distinction. I find myself lost, wandering up and down a block looking for the Globe Café (I am two crucial streets away from it, but I don't know this). I stop people and ask, Do you speak English? and they shake their heads and smile. Diky, I call after them, diky, diky. Diky for nothing!

We go to Roxy, we go to FX.

Grunge, announces Hal, hit Prague like a soggy mattress.

He's right. It looks like it's here to stay, in every bar and café we visit. Americans, Americans. Thousands of dollars but they dress as if they're slumming it.

We stand outside the theatres and study the black & white photographs. Scenes from Beckett, Anouilh, Ionesco. Seriousness. Raised fists. Absurdity. We laugh.

We come across a candles-and-flowers shrine commemorating the Velvet Revolution. There are poems which we cannot read. Some tourists wander up and stand behind us, at a deferential distance. We don't speak until they are gone. We want them to believe what we briefly believe, that this is our memorial, our pain, our revolution. They back away with the hush of the guilty. We look at each other and we laugh. Hal reads a poem out loud in nonsensical Czech phonetics and we laugh again.

We're hungover at Segafredo and I'm cross because they don't have hangover food. I order a hot chocolate without cream.

The waitress doesn't understand me.

Without cream, I say. No cream.

She looks at Hal for help. He finds me embarrassing.

No cream, I say louder. I don't want any cream with the hot chocolate.

She frowns.

Cream? I don't want any?

I mime pouring cream out of a jug. Thick, I mutter.

Her face is blank. She tells me, It does not come with cream.

I make a mental note of this, for next time.

We go to Roxy, we go to Globe, we go to FX.

Look! says Hal. Poetry readings!

We get a cab to FX for the Saturday night poetry reading. The cab driver has a more explicit collection of pornographic pictures than most. I think about what might be in his car boot. He has a high colour and when someone cuts him out at the lights I think I see specks of foam in the corner of his mouth. His moustache makes it hard to be certain. I worry about apoplexy, and how hard it would be to gain control of the car if he were to clutch at his chest and then collapse suddenly around the steering wheel, inert.

We sit in the big armchairs at the back of FX. Some very beautiful women are there. They are all Czech, which is unusual. A – that they're beautiful (no tan stockings encasing ham-like thighs, no tasselled suede pirate boots, no lurid artificial blush applied over undemure cheeks). B – that they are here in FX, which like every other place we go to is usually inhabited by young people from everywhere in the world except Eastern Europe.

Their eyebrows are plucked excruciatingly thin and without exception they have those fashionably swollen big lips. Hal says there must be a special machine in the girls' loos – press a button and a boxing glove pops out and hits you to create that perfect punched-in-the-mouth look. He mimes being hit by it, his head jerking back in a whip-lash movement. Again! I say, clapping my hands together, Again!

The beautiful women drift in and out, past our chairs, talking intently to each other in low voices. Sheets of paper – their poems! – dangle casually from their fingertips.

Czech chicks, murmurs Hal longingly.

Learn the language, I suggest. That'd be a start.

Diky, he says, morose.

Actually I think the language barrier is no bad thing. It provides a lot of scope for meaningful looks. But it does mean that what we understand by a 'poetry reading' is not what the Czechs understand by one – after much quiet and tender-sounding talk between themselves and passing around of the pieces of paper, they stand up and flowingly, waifishly, leave.

We go to Roxy, we go to Roxy.

Hal dances. I don't, won't, can't. The vodka is cheap. It works out, per plastic cup, at 90p. Or a buck and a quarter. Or two dollars fifty. In any currency, it's a cheap shot. Ha ha. Later, we hear that there is some poisoned Polish vodka floating around the city. It was transported from Kracow in rusty vats. More than seven shots a night, the papers say, could kill a grown man. Even so, we do not die.

The receptionist at the hotel says, There is a message for you. We're excited – a message? Who could it be from? Perhaps it is from our friend Louis who is running a bagel factory somewhere outside the city. Perhaps it is news from home, except that nobody knows where we are. Maybe, I think, it could be from the German boy I gave my number to in Chapeau Rouge last night.

But – unhappy travellers! – the message is from the hotel management. We have chipped a corner off the wooden tag attached to our room key.

You have broken this, the message says, and it was new last week. You must replace it.

We are bewildered. I hand over some kroner.

Now? I ask, unsure what to do.

As you wish, the receptionist says, taking my money and giving me a receipt which she first stamps three times.

Sorry about that, we say, and we laugh.

Prague is not a good place to be vegetarian. We go to dinner and order three or four different kinds of meat, which all arrive on the same plate but cooked in different ways. It is a flesh-fest. Hal pretends to adore it but even he is unable to finish the last piece of liver. Vegetables, we say. We want vegetables. When they come they are recently thawed diced things from out of a packet: carrot, sweetcorn, peas. Vodka, we say. We want vodka. Ha ha ha.

Apparently, there are a number of things I do which infuriate Hal. I embarrass him in cafés (the hot chocolate incident); I embarrass him in bars (the German boy incident). I talk too loudly in the street and I can be 'pretentious'. Pretentious, moi? Hal's objections surprise me. We are like an old married couple. He says 'huh' too often (he claims to be unaware of this) and his jaw clicks when he eats. Or is that my father? I can't be sure.

It's too hot in our hotel! The radiators are up full blast. Gusts of warm air chase us down the halls. Our room is a little heat pit. I wake up with gunky eyes and burning sinuses.

The hotel is large. We suspect that there are no other guests. Every now and then – sometimes very early in the morning – we hear the distant whine of a vacuum cleaner on another floor. Who are they vacuuming for? They never vacuum for us. We lie on our beds, stifling in the thick air, rubbing at our sticky eyes. The windows do not open. I decide it is sinister that the windows do not open. After the broken key tag situation it is hard for me to trust the hotel staff. Perhaps the room is bugged. They have our passports, after all. Every night I expect to come back to some fresh damage and another bill for repair. A hole punched in the wall, possibly a broken chair. The suffocating heat does not diminish my unease.

Dear Alicia, I write on a postcard to my sister, We are having a wonderful time in Prague and looking after our hotel room very well. The Czech hospitality is marvellous.

I hand it to the receptionist to post. I smile at her. Diky, post, please, I say. You post?, nodding – Stamp? Diky.

Don't shout, hisses Hal from behind me. You'll ruin everything. You post, I say, please, diky, read it, you silly slav cow, diky.

We make a new friend at the Globe. His name is Dick and he's American. A New Yorker, he tells us, but will later under the influence of vodka admit he is from 'Joisey'. Dick and Hal play backgammon while I write letters I will never send, and drink tumblerfuls of red wine, and listen. Dick's just been in Vietnam.

Oh yeah, he says, it was beautiful. Like going back in time, man. This incredible French architecture, women in long silk pants. Unbelievably cheap, you know, everything. He snickers. And I mean everything.

Hal snickers too. I look at the rain on the Globe's windows and try to imagine Saigon.

We take Dick back to our hotel, where I get changed, and on to the Whale Bar. Vodka, vodka, we cry. Dick pays for everything in American money. In Vietnam, he tells us, he decided to become a dong millionaire. He exchanged however many hundred US dollars into Vietnamese dong, until he had a suitcase filled with great bricks of money. He kept the million dong locked in this suitcase in his hotel room for

a week, not touching it. Then he got crazy on Long Island
Iced Tea one night after this little Spanish senorita he'd been
going with left town. He gambled every last bit of the money
away, ha ha ha, playing poker and twenty-one.

I challenge him to a game of twenty-one, feeling lucky
because it's my age and besides I'm rather good at it, but
Hal cuts in and says I'm not allowed. Dick and Hal both
smile at me, like older brothers, like members of the same
team. What can I do?

Czech chicks! Czech chicks! Hal is getting desperate. It is
difficult for him, travelling with me in tow. He accuses me
of sabotaging all his flirtatious encounters. I can't help it.
Mostly I try not to, but sometimes when he goes to the
bathroom I look at the girl he's been eyeing up and I give
her the evils. I'm only protecting him from himself, after all.
Things got nasty once, in Warsaw. Hal fell in with a bad
crowd, turpentine, death metal, etcetera, and I had to bail
him out. This short Polack girl glommed onto us and
wouldn't leave our hotel. Crying, carrying on. Baby, she
kept saying, baby. Either it was the only English she knew
or it was a serious accusation. Some meat-faced guy who
said he was her brother turned up on the scene, ranting and
raving. Hal didn't like the idea of a big Polish wedding so we
shoved some cigarettes at them and split town. I'm not ready
to leave Prague yet, so Hal will just have to keep himself in
hand. Ha ha ha.

Petrin Hill. What a climb! The heels on my boots stick
into the earth and I skid on wet leaves. Hal has to drag me
up most of the way while Dick strides on ahead. By the time

we're at the top my arms are only just still in their sockets. Something awful happens. Hal doubles over outside the observatory. It could be his back problem. Or it could be liver failure. It makes a good photograph. Aaoow, he says, aaoow. I say cheese while Dick clicks the camera. Tears come out of Hal's eyes. I hold his hands. I feel that I should because some nights he sits on the edge of his bed while I sit on the edge of mine and he holds my hands. (Those are the nights I can't breathe or speak, the nights when the world is spinning way too fast and giving me the shakes. Vodka and cigarettes fail to stop these shakes any more but Hal holding my hands sometimes helps.) It doesn't seem the same rule applies to his back pain. Aaoow, aaoow. Poor baby. I make him lie flat on the damp ground and wipe the sweat off his face. I look around for Dick but he's not there. Help, I shout to the passers-by, Au secours! They keep on passing by. Hal pants and whimpers some more. It hurts to watch him. Then Dick reappears with a hip-flask of whisky. Hal drinks some and shuts his eyes and smiles. His whimpering subsides. He gets to his feet and laughs. What a relief! We love Dick! We jump around. We run all over the top of the hill taking photographs of each other. We are a music video.

Franz Kafka was one skinny guy. Kind of good-looking though. Huh, says Hal, you think so?

He thinks I'm shallow. To prove him wrong I buy a copy of *The Trial*. I will read it soon, right after I've finished *Laughable Loves*.

Dick has hours of fun reading the Police Service note on his street map. 'Dear friends', he shouts to us in a cod Czech accent as we walk up to meet him outside the usual place, 'For the answer to your question, how the crime in Prague differs from the crime in other European cities, it is possible to say: in no way!'

Or, hysterically, in Whale he will tell the barman, 'In the number of committed criminal acts counted for 100,000 inhabitants the Czech Republic is in the order after the Netherlands, Germany, Austria and Switzerland. Therefore Prague is a quiet oasis basically.'

He has memorized it. Hal groans and wrinkles his nose but I could listen to it over and over again.

Dick also likes to remind us that, 'Prague has street prostitutes, too. You can see them in Prelova Street and in a part of Narodni Street. We do not recommend to contact them.'

Hal and Dick have left me alone! Meanies. They've gone 'out on the town' and didn't let me go with them. You better not leave the hotel, they said to me. It's not safe for a young girl alone in the big city.

Life is a cabaret, old chum, they sing as they swing down the stairs of the hotel, leaving me standing forlorn in the doorway, calling out, We do not recommend to contact them. We do NOT recommend it.

I go to Whale, I go to Roxy.

At Roxy I am drinking vodka and not dancing. I am wearing tight Lycra and am highly groomed in order to stand out from the babydoll T-shirts, grubby denim and ornamental hairclips around me. I look fantastique. A boy of I guess about seventeen makes eyes at me. I make eyes back. Then I ignore him, kind of cool. He walks past me. He has a nice body. He turns and smiles at me. I smile back. He walks back past me the other way. I laugh into my vodka. He beckons me to come and sit with him and his friends. I saunter over.

Hi, I say.

Hi, they say. One of them lights my cigarette.

Are you having becher? says the one about to go to the bar. They are Czech! This is perfect. It is cultural relations. Foreign affairs. They buy me drinks even though the money I nicked from Hal's secret supply at the hotel would probably pay their rent for a month. They are economics students.

After the revolution, the one who is still making eyes at me explains, we all wanted to be businessmen. Yuppies. They laugh at this, and I laugh too. Now they would all rather be poets. It is more romantic. But they've enrolled in their courses and they must finish them, or their parents would be disappointed. They ask me what I do and I tell them nothing. They are jealous. They are stoned.

This grass, my boyfriend says, is extra strong. Do you know why? It is because of the acid rain that rained down on all the plants after Chernobyl. The acid gets into the dope and makes it extra strong.

I stifle a yawn.

The friends go to dance and leave me alone with my boyfriend. He has a beautiful smile and a slow blink so I kiss him.

That'll show Hick and Dal.

The Hunger Wall. So-called because at the time it was built there was great poverty. Those men who worked on the wall were guaranteed food. Therefore they did not go hungry. Therefore it was a good thing to heave boulders up to the top of Petrin Hill for days on end. Without machinery or anything. Oh! it is too sad. Aaoow. We carve our initials into one of the rocks with my boyfriend's Swiss Army Knife. It is a gesture of solidarity.

Prague 3 contains student accommodation. I know this because I spend a night there, even though I am no student. I stay in the dorm, in an empty room vacated by a friend of my boyfriend's for the night. We stay there together and I wish I could remember more of it but the truth is I don't. I do remember that he says, You are the first older woman I am with (he is eighteen; I am twenty-one). He also says, I suppose you have read *Unbearable Lightness of Fucking Being*. And, When I have a girlfriend my studies go well and my room is tidier. He spent last summer in New York – actually in Queens, working in a Greek restaurant. It did not improve his English. He says, I know the black slang – fuck you, motherfucker. I laugh. He is nice. He is sweet. He blinks slowly and he waits for a taxicab with me in the morning. You should take the tram, he says, which is a million kroner cheaper than a taxi, but I have never taken a tram in this city before and I am not going to start now. It is enough of a struggle to get back to where the hotel is and find Hal and Dick without this tram business. He kisses me goodbye and

I cry in the taxicab because I am lost and he was nice and sweet and I am not sure where I am going to find Dick and Hal and what sort of mood they will be in when finally I do.

Places where Hal and Dick are not. They are not at the hotel. They are not at Globe. They are not at FX. I think I see them on Charles Bridge but it is not them, just two Australians who look worried when I cry. I have to find them. Whale. Globe. FX. I even go to Chapeau Rouge but it's too early and there's nobody there but the bar staff and a girl smoking a pipe. (It is a good look, and one to consider adopting later.) Where could they be? I ring the hotel and when the receptionist hears me talking she hangs up. I am lost in a city where I don't speak the language and I can't find my only two friends in the whole world. This must be the price of casual sex – my eighteen-year-old, whose name I didn't ever quite hear properly. I need somebody to hold my hands.

In Vietnam, Dick told us, there are beggars who bang their heads on the ground, harder and harder until you pay them to stop.

In Chapeau Rouge again I find them. They have not been back to the hotel. They are still on their bender. Welcome to the lost weekend, they tell me. You naughty, naughty girl, what are you doing out of your room? Dick has two Swedish girls on his arm and Hal is sulking. He is out of Marlboros and is smoking the local brand which he complains is ripping his throat to shreds. Dick has been beating him at backgammon, drinking and girls. I tell them what I've been doing and they berate me for half an hour about the dangers of unknown boys, unknown drugs, unknown addresses and unprotected sex. I didn't mean to tell them about that bit but I'm so happy to have found them I don't care.

Don't care was made to care, Hal tells me.

Yes, says Dick. Don't care was hung.

We have to see Dick to the airport. I don't like city airports, always on the edge of town past flat rust-coloured buildings and low trees. I don't like seeing so much asphalt all in one place. Big airport hotels. Hangars, and shuttle buses. Rental car places. Corrugated iron manufacturers. I know it's not fashionable to think nature is beautiful and that these man-made monstrosities are a waste of space. You're so un-modern, Hal will say. This is the future, this is real. You are such a girl.

We all cry a little, saying good-bye. Well, we make the sounds of crying and that's enough. Dick is going to Kingston, Jamaica. My heart is down, he sings, My head is spinning around.

But that's the leaving Kingston song, I say, not the leaving Prague song.

There is no leaving Prague song, he says, because I am too bowed with grief for music.

Oh, I sigh, and feel a single tear running down my cheek.

Huh, says Hal.

Goodbye, says Dick.

Au revoir! Au revoir!

To comfort ourselves we take a walk by the river. It is grey, and glimmering (it never stops glimmering). We see a man fishing down a grating with a hat out to collect money. There is slightly too much of this sad-eye clown culture in Prague, if you ask me. Paintings on velvet, puppets on string – that sort of thing.

Take my picture, I tell Hal.

I pose next to the fishing clown and look mournful. We have six rolls of black & white film. It is très romantique. Me on the Charles Bridge, me with the Vltava in the back-ground, me in front of the cathedral. Très Juliette Binoche. We don't take photographs of Hal. Il est trop laide. We did take some of Dick, Dick and me in pornographic contortions in our hotel room. We can sell them to the taxi drivers if we ever run out money. This won't happen. Not as long as we stay in Eastern Europe.

What are you feeling, Hal asks me, surprisingly, back at the hotel. What are you feeling? F.e.e.l.i.n.g.

I shrug, giggling.

Search me!

Hal can sniff out an exhibition opening at twenty paces, in any city. They are the same the world over, unlike poetry readings. The tricky part is timing it so's you're not conspic-uous out-of-towners, but not getting there so late that all the free drink is gone. We throw back as much as we can, look at the art a bit, and leave. This show involves a lot of perspex and fluorescent light. It's conceptual. We don't understand the concept. There is a cultural divide.

Hal is losing patience with my spouting of inside knowl-edge of the Czech people, gleaned from the night I spent with my sex slav. He accuses me of trying to make the best

of a botched situation. Yes?, I say, not sure quite what is
wrong with that. It comes out that he is still cross with me
for doing it, that he thinks I took a stupid risk, that he
believes 'it's different for girls', i.e. worse, and that as he's
responsible for me I should respect his wishes. Then he
actually says, 'act your age not your shoe size'. Excuse me?
Hello? He can't tell me to grow up. I'm twenty-one. I am
grown up! But I do shut up, mainly because I've repeated
everything the sex slav and his friends told me and everything I've read in *Laughable Loves* (which after all is fiction,
and quite old) and I've run out of inside knowledge about
the Czech culture. Damn.

I miss Dick. No amount of cajoling or wheedling would
persuade him to delay his ticket. Have I been let down by
him? Yes. Has he used me? It's dawning on me that, most
probably, he has. It's not that I thought it was love or
anything, I just felt like – we had a special bond. The time
when we snuck away from Hal and ate sausages in Wenceslas
Square, and Dick said that Prague was the most romantic
city in the world and I held my breath, then had to let it out
after a minute because nothing happened ... The times
when I'm sure I caught him looking at me in a certain kind
of way ... The enthusiasm he showed for our dirty photo
session ... I could have been wrong. I must have been too
gullible. I have no instinct about Dick. Perhaps I'll get back
to the hotel and find a one-way ticket to Jamaica waiting for
me. It's possible, after all; anything is possible!

I can see myself marrying someone like Dick – I can
imagine the wedding, the honeymoon, the drink and the

infidelities. The reconciliations, the anti-depressants, the
children and the diets. The trial separations, the therapy.
Dick reminds me of Robert Wagner. The glamour.

Huh, says Hal, when I confess my marital fantasy over
vodkas at HP (a mistake, both the venue and the confession),
You've been reading too many novels. And now I am
confused because the old argument used to be that I didn't
read enough! Hal is hard to please. I tell him so – it seems
to please him.

How long is it since I've seen the sea? I wake up,
adrenaline racing through me. Hal, I say, Hal, how far away
from the ocean are we? He snores and rolls over. We have a
map. I dig it out of the suitcase and spread it over my bed.
In the faint light I can make out where we are. Then
Hungary, Romania, Black Sea. Austria, Italy, Adriatic Sea.
Germany, Netherlands, North Sea. Poland, Baltic Sea – the
shortest route. We're surrounded on all sides. The room is
extra hot. My hands are prickling. I don't want the river. I
don't want some dead old spa town or a lake. I want the
ocean, the Pacific Ocean. The new world. This never-ending
stone oppresses me. The cobbled streets, the ruins, the
ancient tombs – it's all so much dust. You can have it. It
smells like decay and chalk. Boulders being carried up
mountains. Wake up, Hal, wake up.

Hey, says Hal, I know. Let's change all our money and
become zloty millionaires. Ha ha ha.

I'd rather be travelling with the fishing clown than be
travelling with this. I mean it.

I thought I saw Dick today, in the little café on the steps

above the castle. We'd been looking at the tomb of Vladimir the Torturer, or whatever his name is. Again. Crypt after crypt, monument after monument, one fascinating piece of history after another. The guy I thought was Dick was actually the tour guide. You never know.

An old American man who has been hitting on me follows us out of Chapeau Rouge. Gross. He's forty at least. He totters along the street after us while we giggle, ignoring him. He's muttering something. We stop so we can hear what it is. He catches up with us, looks confused as if he's trying to remember where he knows us from. I lean towards him, into the mutter.

Is Roxy open. Is Roxy open. Is Roxy open.

This is what he has to say.

We walk through Unpronounceable Square for breakfast at Cornucopia.

What do you want to do today? asks Hal.

Go to the beach, I say.

Ha ha ha.

We go shopping. I buy a beret and Hal buys a fridge magnet, though we do not own a fridge. We walk up to the Globe, we read English magazines and play backgammon. We drink coffee and all the time I'm thinking the sea, the sea. The white light of home, the smell of salt and coconut oil, hot rubber and woodsmoke. Summer music from a car stereo. Roller blades and pohutukawa flowers, green hills and the green horizon of the sea.

You are as drunk as a rainbow. That's another thing the sex Slav said to me, that I'd forgotten. I'm not quite sure what it means – only, I suppose (an educated guess) that you are very, very drunk.

I am sick in the toilet at Roxy. I splash my face with cold water the way men do and tell myself it's only motion sickness.

'Pickpockets', Dick was fond of telling me, 'prefer to work in a tight squeeze. It arises especially in department stores.' Then he'd kiss my cheek. Just remember that, honey, he'd say, they like nothing more than a tight squeeze. Ha ha ha. Diky, Dick.

Do you understand, says Hal, holding my hands in the hot hotel room, that we can't go back yet?

My teeth are chattering.

Look at me, he says. Do. You. Understand.

He waits. I nod my head, yes.

OK, he says. OK. Tomorrow we'll take the train to Budapest. Smile!

We go to Budapest. We go.

# running around with you

Helen and Idiot set to sea
In a beautiful pea-green boat.

Idiot's eaten by a shark
And Helen fails to float.

They fell in love, or so she later claimed, during a power cut at a party. It was very early morning. Most of the guests would have left if it wasn't for a torrential summer rainstorm that had started outside. There was a high wind with it and somewhere down the road a tree was blown over on to power lines. All the lights in the street went out. At the party the music stopped. A couple of women squealed. A collective 'oooh' went up, as though someone had thrown the switch to give a secret signal and now something exciting was going to happen.

Standing by the large doors that opened out on to the garden, Helen knew too that something was about to happen. She was pleasantly unsteady on her feet, full of vermouth and gin. How nice to be in a room full of strangers, the lights out, the rain streaking the garden. The shitty day she'd had – waiting for a phone call that never came and being too morbid to get dressed – swiftly rewrote itself. Now it seemed to have all been part of the build-up to this romantic moment – lying on the couch in her petticoat reading, the silence of the hot afternoon. She forgot that Trudi had had to persuade her to come to this party, that she'd dressed out of revenge on her ex-boyfriend and drunk too much once she got here. She forgot that Trudi had taken her aside before leaving the party and said, Be Careful. She forgot that a minute ago she'd thought, I have nothing to say to these people. It was all part of this, this significant moment. Hadn't she felt a sense of something important? Hadn't the day's blankness just been part of the preparation for this? She took a deep breath and felt filled with romantic potential. Right, she said to herself, looking at the thrashing trees, her back to the room. Right. The next man I lay eyes on will be the love of my life.

Helen woke in Eliot's bed the morning after the party. She was at a loss as to how to behave. Nerves overcame her, made worse by the fact that Eliot still resembled her ex-boyfriend in the light of day. She lay awake and gave the situation some thought. The only thing to do was to leave. While she was looking for her clothes Eliot woke up.

—Hi, he said.

—Hi, she said, looking at the floor. She really shouldn't be expected to converse with him. Couldn't he just pretend to be asleep like normal people do?

—You going?

—Yeah. She paused by the mirror to put fresh lipstick on, enjoying the studied nonchalance. There wasn't going to be any explaining herself. Let him figure it out.

He laughed.

—What? she asked, coy, waiting for the compliment.

—I was just remembering what you said last night.

—What did I say?

—You don't remember? He laughed again.

—No. Helen smiled a tight smile. She picked her coat up off the floor and made herself look at him.

—Bye then.

—See you, he said, staring at her.

—Sure, she said, trying not to sound as if she meant it too much. —See you.

She let herself out of the house, past the bicycles and rubbish, and stood in the windy street with her hands over her eyes groaning with embarrassment. She wondered how the hell she was going to get home. The front door to his house opened and he stood on the step with a towel around his waist.

—Hey, he said, and she turned to him, her eyes huge with awkwardness, —can I get your phone number?

She smiled a bit and blushed a bit and told him. He repeated it twice, fixing her with a stare so intense it looked like he practised it in front of the mirror. He said he'd see her soon. She looked at her feet and nodded and said OK. He shut the door and she walked up the road for five minutes before she realised she was going in the wrong direction.

The crucial factor being that not once, in any of the few words she said that first morning, did Helen use her normal voice. The voice that came out of her mouth was soft, slow and husky. A cross between a Dynasty whisper and Jessica Rabbit. A voice to seduce Eliot with. A voice to say 'so long' with as she stood over the dead body of her ex-boyfriend, the gun in her hand still smoking. A voice for all occasions, but only one mood. A voice like a suit of armour, a voice to wear to a masked ball.

Eliot is new to the city and works on a style magazine. Helen is impressed by this despite herself. Oh yeah, she likes to say, he works for Cyburbia. It's pretty cutting edge. She neglects to mention that his job is putting the listings column together. When he goes off to the magazine she says she is spending the day 'working' in the library. Sometimes it's true. He thinks she has a research grant. He doesn't need to know about the small inheritance from her grandmother that is enough for the rent and food and clothes and buys her time while she decides what she really wants to do with her life. Besides, she does spend a lot of time in the library, photocopying chapters out of books she decides are interesting and staring into space. If asked, she is 'putting together some background material' for a 'screenplay – well, possibly not a screenplay but at the moment I feel film is the right medium for what I want to say.' She 'doesn't want to be precious about it' but she'd 'rather not discuss it. I'm hopelessly inarticulate about it' (self-deprecating smile). Meanwhile, her desk drawer becomes gratifyingly full with 'material'. She's thinking about investing in a box-file.

The first few weeks she is seeing Eliot, Helen spends a lot of time on the phone to her friends.

—I definitely like him, she says. —He's so nice. Not boring nice, but nice nice. Funny. He's so funny. You'd like him.

—He sounds great, says Holly or Trudi or Janet or Bill.

—Oh, he is, he really is.

—When are we going to meet him?

—Soon, she says, thinking she should get off the phone in case he's trying to ring through. —Soon.

She holds back until he leaves for work in the morning and after looking at the ceiling for a while she picks up the phone again.

—He is so funny, he was so sweet last night. I think he really likes me. We went for a drive and we didn't say anything the whole time. We don't have to talk. It's so comfortable.

—He sounds great.

—Yeah, he is.

—Really looking forward to meeting him.

—Mmm.

Sometimes she can't even wait till he is out of the house to ring them.

—He's in the kitchen making dinner. Isn't that perfect? I think I'm in a relationship. I mean, I really am. I can't believe it. He can cook. Thank God, because I can't boil an egg. You should really meet him.

—Yeah, right.

—What are you doing on Saturday night? Eliot's going

out for a boy's night with some guy from his work, you know, Cyburbia. Are you guys doing anything?

—God, I'd love to know what you're thinking, Eliot says in bed one night.

Helen can't think of anything interesting to say. —Why? she asks, rolling away self-consciously.

—I just can't figure you out.

—Maybe there's nothing to figure, she says, with enough smoke in her voice to make it sound like a lie.

—You're such an enigma.

—Really? reaching lazily for a glass of water.

—Like a cat.

—I don't think that's a compliment, Eliot.

—I love cats.

She puts the glass back on the night table and smiles at him.

—Meow.

She does feel a little bit bad, knowing how bogus her Mystery Woman act really is. But it's so much more fun than just being her. And so much easier. So she continues to be a mixture of shy and aloof, to speak English as if it was her second or third language, and to gaze out of the window at appropriate moments. Eliot can't get enough. The only problem is her stupid friends. If they see her acting like this they'll just laugh.

—Helen, says Bill, the third time she calls to cancel an arrangement, —why are you so cagey about me meeting Eliot?

—I'm not, she says, —really, it's just this work thing came up for him and—

—You are so, you have been completely cagey about it ever since you guys got together.

—Well, to be honest, Bill, I thought it might be a bit awkward. Not you but him. I mean, you're a guy, you know how they get – possessive, or—

—But you've kept him away from everyone, not just me. Trudi says you've cancelled twice on her as well.

—Oh, so now you guys are discussing this? My friends get together and have Why-can't-we-meet-Eliot sessions? Form a support group, Bill, I mean really.

—Look, all I'm saying is, if you don't want us to meet him, fine. If he's some hunchback bogeyman you're ashamed to be seen with in public, that's great. But just say it, don't do this crazy Eliot's-working-late behaviour.

—He's not a weirdo, it's nothing like that.

—Then what is it?

—Well, you know, it's early days. I just don't know if I'm ready for my worlds to collide yet, OK.

—Fine. Cool. I can understand that. Just give us a call when you're feeling up to it, all right?

—Promise.

The conversation with Trudi is not dissimilar, except that she has obviously already been primed by Bill.

—What I want to know is, if he's not a gross-out and you're not embarrassed of him, then who are you embarrassed of? Us?

—Yes, Trudi, for eight years I've been meaning to tell you how mortifying it is to hang out with you.

—No, but are you? Is he like some Mr Coolie who's going to think we're a bunch of losers? You know, because we're not hip enough?

—No, he's not like that at all.

—Good, because I was going to say, if he is like that how does he stand being with you? Ha ha ha.

—Ha ha ha, Tru, says Helen.

Eliot's curiosity about Helen is insatiable. He wants to know everything there is to know about her. Sometimes he watches her when she's not aware of it, and she'll give a little sigh, or look pensive, or laugh to herself and he just knows there's something really interesting going on there. He doesn't know what it is – she doesn't like to talk about herself at all – but this just makes him more interested, more certain of her depths, more desperate to plumb them. She'll trust him soon enough. Meanwhile, he lies awake at night, hoping she'll talk in her sleep and let something slip.

—I'm moving, Helen tells Bill.

—Where?

—In with Eliot.

—You've got to be joking.

—I knew you'd be like this.

—You've known him how long?

—Long enough. A month or something. It's the right thing to do, Bill, please don't give me any grief over this.

—OK.

—So do you think it's a good idea?


Helen watches Eliot eating. He chews with his mouth closed. He chews everything a lot of times. He holds his knife and fork precisely the right way. She's going to see this every single day. She'd better get used to it.

—When am I going to see some of your screenplay?

—Oh, Eliot, she laughs in her sexy husky Kathleen Turner fake way. —When it's ready.

—Can't I even see some work in progress? I could show it to Tanya at the magazine. Her boyfriend works at the Film Commission. We could get you some more money.

—It's not ready yet, darling. She's smiling through gritted teeth. Drop it, you fuck, she's thinking, just drop it. Eliot brings the salad to the table, looks at her lovingly.

—What's going on behind those green eyes of yours?

—Oh, just thinking about the main character, she says, —the hero. He's walked into something he shouldn't have and I'm wondering if I'm going to have to kill him off.


She has to take him to the opening of Trudi's exhibition because he saw the invitation lying on the kitchen table. Careless of her. Trudi had scrawled Bring Eliot on it.

—Great, said Eliot, I'd love to go, meet some of your friends.

He only saw the invite the day before the opening. He didn't say, When exactly were you planning to tell me about this? She wonders if he even thought it.

So here they are, drinking cask wine and not being allowed to smoke, talking to Bill. Helen's story is that she has a cold, which explains why her voice is so low and husky – she managed to convince Bill of this while Eliot was looking at the paintings. Who goes to a gallery opening to look at the work? Sometimes he is such a hick.

—So what do you think, Eliot? Bill asks.

Jesus, thinks Helen. This'll be embarrassing.

—I like it, Eliot says slowly. —I like this one a lot. I'm not sure if I get all of them, though.

Helen snorts.

—I'd say that's probably a good thing, says Bill. —There's a lot of chick stuff here.

—Oh, laughs Eliot, —is that what it is? Helen, I never knew.

Bill laughs too while Helen gives them the finger.

—God, that girl art thing, says Bill, —we're not *supposed* to get it, Eliot, for Christ's sake.

—Oh right, says Eliot, —'cause we're just dumb guys, I forgot. Duh.

—Hey, look, says Bill, pointing to one painting. —I think I see a vagina.

—Nah, says Eliot, —it's a tampon, stupid.

They're killing themselves.

—Good that you crack each other up, Helen glowers.

Eliot's making an effort, Helen can see that, but she still can't relax. Bill's only humouring him, Helen is sure. He can tell Eliot really is just a dumb guy. And Eliot's niceness, his damn affability which seemed so refreshing when they first met, now makes her want to poke sharp sticks at him.

—Great work, she says, kissing Trudi. —I love that dress.

—Thanks for coming babe, says Trudi. —What's wrong with your voice?

Eliot looks confused.

—Got a cold, Helen mutters. Shit.

—I'm Eliot, says Eliot, —I really like your paintings.

Trudi dimples at him. —Eliot, at last. Hel's told me so much about you.

She takes his arm and steers him towards the drinks' table.

Helen watches helplessly, seething.

—Don't be so paranoid, says Bill, —I'm the one who's supposed to feel marginalized in here, not you.

—Don't be ridiculous, says Helen.

—He's a great guy, says Bill. —I can't imagine what you're worried about. Trudi knows it's hands off.

Helen doesn't like Bill's tone. —You try to simplify things by making them complicated, she says.

—Who are you, he laughs, —Barbara Kruger?

She curls her lip at him. No, she thinks glumly, looking at her empty glass and over to Eliot and Trudi by the wine, more like Freddy Krueger.

She tries to stay at least within earshot of Eliot. God knows what either of them could be saying. At one point she hears her name and lunges over, grabs Eliot and asks him if he wants to go out for a cigarette.

—Oh, smoke in here, says Trudi, —no one gives a shit.

—Well, we really have to get going anyway.

—Aren't you coming out for dinner? We've booked a table.

Eliot looks at Helen. No, she thinks, this is enough for one night. I can't take any more of it.

—I'd love to, Tru, but I'm so tired.

—Really? Eliot, why don't you come anyway?

Just try it, thinks Helen.

—Oh, no thanks. Not if Hel's too tired. Another time though. I'll just get the coats.

Trudi watches him as he walks away. She smiles. —You've got him well-trained.

Helen smiles too, sweetly. —Have you sold any work tonight?

—There's a lot of interest, says Trudi, lighting a cigarette. —But no, not exactly.

Helen lets Eliot help her into her coat, happier now she's got Trudi on the back foot. —Well, it really is a good show, I'm sure someone will buy something.

Eliot nods. —Yeah, it's great to meet you finally.

—See you soon, says Trudi, —I hope.

—Better go, mutters Helen.

—Don't leave me, Eliot, says Bill, —I feel so alien, so other. I'm surrounded by curious symbolic holes—

Eliot shakes Bill's hand. Helen winces. —Take it like a man, he says. —Hey, I'll give you a call – we can go for a drink somewhere butch.

—That'd be cool. Helen's got my number. See you, Hel. I won't kiss you. Don't want to catch that cold.

—The thing I hate is, Helen would say to Trudi in the old days, —guys are scared of me.

Then she'd pause.

—Or they're too stupid to know they should be.

One time Trudi asked her what exactly she meant. Helen had shrugged, not knowing how to say that she wasn't sure. Not knowing how to admit that she just liked the way it sounded.

—How's Idiot? says Bill.

—That's not his name, Bill, says Helen, thinking Only I'm allowed to call him that.

—I wasn't talking about Eliot.

—Don't be a shit.

—Helen, why don't we ever see you any more?

—You do.

—When?

—Oh, you know – the other night at that thing—

—You were there for all of five minutes and then you whisked Eliot away. I just don't understand why you're avoiding me. There's a small silence. Helen looks at the ceiling and chews her lip.

—Bill, I'm not 'avoiding' you. I'm really busy and I'm in a new relationship. We've just moved in together, I want to spend some time on that. Why are you suddenly making all these demands?

Helen knows she's overstepping the line here but she can't help it, she's sick of having to defend herself to Bill and everyone, surely she has a right to do what the hell she wants.

—OK, fine. I'm not making demands, Helen. I just want to see you sometimes. I'm your friend for Christ's sake.

—I know, darling, it's just I feel so bullied sometimes—

—By me? You feel bullied by me?

—Well, sometimes—

There's another, longer silence.

—OK, Helen. You call me when you want to.

—Bill, I don't mean—

He's hung up.

Helen lights a cigarette.

—So, she says to the empty room, —why should I have to—

But she doesn't finish the sentence. The cigarette tastes disgusting. She mashes it out.

—I'm so happy with you, Jessica Rabbit's voice says to Idiot that night.

—Me too, says Idiot.


Helen is waxing her legs in the kitchen when the phone rings. It's Eliot, calling from the magazine.

—What are you up to?

—Working, she says. —I'm about to go into the library.

The wax is going to dry too hard on her legs before she has a chance to rip it off.

—How's it going?

—Fine, she says, unable to keep the irritation out of her voice. —Why are you ringing?

—Sorry, I've interrupted you. I was thinking, maybe we should have a dinner party.

—What for?

—For our friends. Well, for your friends. I'd like to get to know them. I've been here six months and I still don't know anyone apart from the people at work and you.

That's not my problem, she thinks. —I don't know. I don't like dinner parties.

—Or drinks maybe.

—Mm.

—I'm sorry, this is a bad time, isn't it. You go back to your work. We'll talk about it later.

Great, thinks Helen, another conversation to avoid having.

—OK, sure. I've got to go.

—Love you.

—Bye.

She has to rinse the wax off in the shower. What am I doing, she thinks. What am I doing?

—I met a friend of yours today, says Eliot as they're getting ready to go out.

Helen stops mid-lipstick. —What?

She notices how strange her lips look half-red, the natural colour drained from them. She quickly smudges them together and raises her eyebrows.

—Who was it?

—A guy, dark hair – uh . . .

No, she's thinking, not the ex, please not the ex. This would be a disaster.

—Uh, Grant, or something.

—Grant? she echoes, her whole body tingling with relief. —Who's Grant, she wonders out loud.

—Well, he knew you.

—How? She's managing to keep her hands still enough to do eyeshadow now, and keep an eye on Eliot through the mirror as he sits on the bed buttoning his shirt.

—He said he knew you from the theatre.

—What theatre? Helen is confused.

—That's what I said. I didn't know you were involved in the theatre.

—I wasn't, she says, laughing a shade too unnaturally. A case of mistaken identity. She can make this one work for her. She turns to him and laughs again, —Can you imagine? Me! It must have been a mistake.

—Well, I don't know – he saw the photograph of you I've got on my noticeboard, he definitely seemed to recognize you.

Eliot's catching on. The guy must have known Helen, this is part of the past she's so mysterious about. Now she's trying to cover it up.

—Look, darling, it couldn't have been me, I've hardly been near a theatre in my life. It must have been some actress he knows. Some actress, she thinks, hearing the applause in her mind. She sprays perfume around her neck, wishing she had one of those big scent puffers to complete the *All About Eve* image.

—I suppose so, says Eliot. —He knew your name.

The guy hadn't actually been able to remember what the actress was called, but when Eliot said 'Helen' he thought it sounded about right.

—My surname?

—No. But he knew you were called Helen.

This was getting more surreal by the minute. Whoever this guy was, he couldn't have done a better job of increasing Helen's intrigue quotient if she'd been paying him.

—Well, Helen's not that uncommon. It must be some other girl. Do you think I'd lie about it? She laughs again, tinkling, dangerous. She's reminding him of their unspoken agreement. Don't push too far or she might walk.

—Of course not, he says, though more slowly than he should.

—Well then, she smiles, —you can ask him next time you see him if he's quite sure.

—Yes, says Eliot, but the guy was just visiting the magazine for one meeting and wasn't likely to be coming back. —Yes, I might. He looks at Helen, her make-up perfect. —Shall we go then?

—Yes, let's, she says, barely able to restrain herself from blowing a kiss to the mirror. —I'm starving.

Eliot has lunch with two girls from the magazine. He goes to the counter to order more coffee and when he comes back they are in the middle of a conversation about sex.

They keep talking as if he isn't there. At first he's insulted but he gradually becomes fascinated, not with what they're saying – that women discuss sex with each other terrifies him – but by the way they are talking. The short-haired one is laughing and waving her arms around as she describes some incident to the dark-haired girl, who is nodding and sucking on a cigarette as if she needs it to keep breathing. She interrupts constantly with questions or 'no's' or 'Jesus Christ's'. They seem so animated, so alive. Eliot finds himself trying to imagine Helen like this. She certainly isn't ever like this with him.

—Sorry, Eliot, the short-haired girl says, —this is terribly rude, it's just girl stuff.

He mumbles something about, Don't mind me, but he really wants to say, Don't stop, keep going, I could watch you all afternoon. They sit in uncomfortable silence for a minute or two before the bill arrives and they can talk about that.

When Eliot turns his key in the front door that evening he feels overcome by a sense of claustrophobia. He can feel Helen's secrecy enveloping him like musky perfume, dazing and numbing him like a drug. She's got to open up to him soon. She's just got to.

—Are you happy? says Eliot.

What sort of question is that, thinks Helen. —Yes, she says, uncertainly.

—I think we should go away for this weekend. The country.

They drive in their usual silence for three or four hours to the cottage Eliot has borrowed from his boss at Cyburbia.

Helen's agoraphobia sets in as soon as they pass through the last suburbs of the city but she keeps quiet about it.

—Isn't this beautiful? says Eliot as they unpack their things from the car. He kisses her on the nose. —Just the two of us, alone together for the whole weekend.

Helen doesn't think there's anything so unusual about that. She wipes the top of her nose when he's not looking.

She has to admit it's pretty nice though, drinking red wine while Eliot cooks pasta over the old stove. They light candles, a fire. Etcetera. The bed is old and creaky.

—This is nice.

—Happy? says Eliot.

—Mmm, says Helen. —Happy.

The next day is wet. Eliot is quite content inside, playing cards and reading. Helen looks out the window a lot. Cabin fever.

—I might go for a walk.

—It's raining.

—Yeah, that's OK. So what, Helen wants to say to just about everything that comes out of Eliot's mouth these days. So fucking what?

—Helen . . . He looks up. If he wore glasses he would take them off at this point. —We need to talk.

Helen feels her stomach drop. —Why?

He keeps looking at her, steady, even. —You know why.

—Uh, no.

He stands up and pours a cup of tea, shakily. He laughs

badly, nervously. —I mean, what do I have to do to get you to properly talk to me? Withold sexual favours?

She looks at the floor, giving herself some time. This is no threat. She'll get around him. She always does.

—Eliot. She sighs. She goes to him and takes his hand. —There are just—some things— she looks away, biting her lip, —I'm not ready to talk about yet. I'm trying, she says, feeling with surprise her eyes pricking with tears, —I really am. I'm trying to be brave—. She turns away, one hand over her mouth.

—Oh, Hel, he says. —Oh, I'm so sorry. I should never have rushed you like this.

He puts his arms around her from behind and she lets herself lean back into him with a teary sigh. —I'm sorry, he says. —I love you.

She turns towards him and presses her cheek to his shoulder. She lets him feel what a fragile little thing she is, fragile and vulnerable, only just learning to trust.

—I'm going to go for a walk.

He looks down into her eyes, full of remorse and concern. —I'll come with you.

—No, she says, smiling weakly, —I'll just be a little while.

She leaves him there in the warm cabin and walks through the rain marvelling at her own capacity for pretence. She comes to the local shops and has a cup of bad coffee in the smelly tea-rooms. She'll let him stew for a while and then go back. She looks around, white bread sandwiches curling at the corners, formica table-tops sticky with tomato sauce spills. Perhaps she could disappear in a place like this, rent a cottage on her own and just drop out of life. Write her screenplay. Marry the village idiot. Wait a minute she thinks, spooning crusty sugar into her cup. I am the village idiot. Or one of us is.

Eliot announces excitedly that his old friend Andrew is passing through town, and they can all go out for dinner. Cool, thinks Helen, the girlfriends get to talk to each other while the guys bond. Neat. But it's something to do, and Eliot is obviously looking forward to it so much that she agrees to go. Bad move. Should have stayed at home.

—I can't believe you were so rude.

Eliot yanks the fridge door open. A carton of milk falls out and spills on to the floor.

—I'll get it, says Helen, sitting down and lighting a cigarette.

—Oh shit. He drags a cloth over it. —Jesus, Helen, they are my friends.

—Well, they're fucking awful.

—Shut up.

—Do you want to know why? she laughs, —do you want a list?

—No, just shut up. I don't want to even speak to you.

—You're drunk.

—So are you. He stands staring into the fridge, his back to her.

—One. I have never heard a man go on about 'fucking

fags' so much in one evening. In one lifetime even. Two.
That girlfriend of his had the world's most irritating laugh.
Three. They're completely self-obsessed. Four.

—Shut up, Helen, I'm telling you.

—Four. He was a racist, sexist, homophobic shit. Five.
He was unspeakably rude to me . . .

Eliot nearly choked. —Don't even pretend to be surprised
about that. You rolled your eyes every time he asked you a
question. And then you lectured him about the way he . . .

—That's another thing – he snapped his fingers at the
waitress. That is so low . . .

—All right. All right. Shut up. Yes, you're right. He's a
bigot. I'm not blind. I did notice. Don't flick your ash on the
floor.

—You'd have to be dead not to notice.

—But he is my oldest friend, Helen, I don't know any
people here remember – it just would have been nice to see
him without you glaring over the table the whole night.
Eliot passes Helen an ashtray.

—Why is he your friend? He's a screaming asshole. She
flicks her ash on the table.

—If you hadn't steered the conversation back to fucking
politics every five minutes it would have been all right. Since
when have you been Little Miss PC anyway? He was just
winding you up.

—Yes. Because he hates me. Because he's in love with
you.

—Oh, shut up.

But she'd got him. He was trying not to laugh.

—Isn't he? Andrew is in love with you.'Oh, Eliot, remember the time we went camping.' 'Oh, Eliot, remember that hitch-hiking holiday?' Always going on about 'fucking queers' who tried to pick him up. In his dreams. God knows what the two of you used to get up to in your cosy little tent.

—You are so sordid. It's sex sex sex with you isn't it? Eliot throws the cloth in the sink and starts to walk over to her chair.

—Well, it's true. Helen slips off her shoes and smiles up at him. —He couldn't stand the idea that I go to bed with you every night and he can't.

—At least I've got friends.

—I've got friends.

—Right, and we see them all the time.

—That's because I want you all to myself, darling.

—Is it? He slumps into a chair. Exhausted. Drunk. Confused.

—Eliot. She gets up and kneels on the floor next to his chair. —We don't need anybody else. You're all I want. I'm sorry I was horrible tonight. She puts her head on his knee. —Maybe I'm jealous.

—Are you? He doesn't want to touch her but his hand reaches out and strokes her hair. —Are you jealous?

—Mm, she says, a hundred miles away again. —Maybe.


At first Eliot thinks that the filthy mood which has settled on Helen like dust is only a case of bad PMT. But the weeks go by, and the diagnosis stretches to mid-menstrual tension, post-menstrual tension – sometimes he wonders if she's just a grumpy bitch.

—How's the screenplay going? he attempts one night.

—OK, Helen grunts.

—When are you going to let me have a look?

She's silent for so long he wonders if she's heard him.

—Helen?

—What?

—Has it got a title?

—Yeah, she says, —it's called My Stupid Fucking Life.

—God, why are you so—

—So what?

—Nothing. He wishes he'd never started.

—No, what, Eliot, I'm curious.

She's opening a bottle of wine and looking at him with more interest than she's shown in a fortnight.

—Well, so – negative?

—You think I'm negative?

—Yes, I do. He eyes her hand on the bottle opener nervously. It wouldn't be the first time she's thrown something.

She smiles. She pulls the cork out of the bottle. – I'm going to bed, she says. —Are you coming?

Afterwards he says to her, —Sometimes I don't know where you begin and end.

Funny, she thinks, seeing herself lying there as if from the other side of the room. Neither do I.

And so it goes on like this, sex, fight, fight, sex, sex, not talking, etcetera. It's a miracle Eliot's not bored out of his brains, but he's got a pretty high threshold for boredom. He's still so fascinated by the spectacle of Helen that he watches as if she were on a movie screen – she turns, she laughs, she blinks and smiles – Featuring Tonight! Helen H as Femme Fatale! Following her award-winning performance as Bitch From Hell! Part of the Mystery Woman Trilogy! And Eliot sits enthralled, never able to fully understand what makes her work, never once for a minute considering that there might be no more behind the mannerisms than another mannerism.

Helen's birthday. Nobody rings her. No post. No nothing. Oh dear. She goes to dinner with Eliot. They ride out the silences and manage to get on OK. He gives her a book on screen-writing. She bites back the words How fucking romantic. She's making an effort, giving it a go. If she can't say anything nice, blah blah.

She's first through the door at home and races to the answer machine. Nothing. The woman that time forgot. She wonders what exactly it is she's done to herself, and why.

Eliot leaves for Cyburbia the next morning and Helen is working her way up to getting out of bed when the phone rings.

—Helen?

—Hello?

—It's Trudi.

—Tru! Helen sits up in bed.

—How are you?

—OK, she says, suddenly unable to say anything else.

—I haven't heard from you for so long.

Helen finds herself still incapable of speaking. —Mm, she says, hoping Trudi won't hear the tears in her voice. She pinches her leg. —How are you?

—Busy. Really busy. I'm going to China. That's why I'm ringing.

—China, says Helen, nodding, bruising her leg she is gripping it so hard. —Wow.

—I know! Hey are you OK?

—Yeah, I'm fine, Helen says, —hang on a minute.

She runs into the bathroom and blows her nose. She looks at her wet red face for a second and takes a deep breath. Trudi forgot her birthday. Everyone has forgotten her birthday. She doesn't have any friends.

—Sorry, she says, too brightly. —The toast was burning.

—Get you, having breakfast at ten thirty am. Lucky for some. Hey, so I'm leaving next week.

—Why are you going? Who would want to go to China anyway, thinks Helen, what a hole.

—I've got a transfer there for a year. Teaching art to schoolkids. I can't believe I'm doing it.

—Sounds great.

—Yeah, well, I'm having a big party this Friday. Can you come?

—Friday? says Helen stupidly, like a teenager who pretends she's got to check her diary.

—At my place. About nine or something. Everyone's going to be there.

—Everyone, says Helen. What has she got, echolalia or something?

—You know, Bill, Holly, Mike, everyone. Trudi laughs. —I'd really love to see you before I go. Bill was asking about you the other day.

—Oh, really? How is he?

—He's great. In love as usual. Some cow who treats him like shit. So listen, what have you been up to? How's Eliot?

—He's great, says Helen, – look, Tru, I've got to go, my other line's bleeping.

—Will you come on Friday?

—Yes, lies Helen, —definitely. I'd love to see you. China, wow. I've got to go.

—OK—

—Have a great time.

—Well, I'll see you Friday, yeah?

—Yes, Friday. OK – bye.

She hangs up before she has to hear Trudi say goodbye. She leans forward and shoves her head into a pillow. She hits her stomach where she can feel the emptiness. She hits it again and again. She lies there for another hour or so, drifting in and out of bad dreams, before she stands up, lost in the late-morning bedroom, face tight from tears, not knowing, not knowing what to do. Then she cleans her teeth and washes Eliot's breakfast dishes. Drinks gin while she is cleaning the house. Its ammonia taste makes her feel as if she, too, is being cleaned out, rinsed over with disinfectant. How to be at one with your bathroom. Bonding with the fridge like the ice princess that she is.

Eliot has taken to doing reckless and stupid things. He gets drunk at home and then goes out driving. He's gone off food. He swears at his boss. Eliot's little bids for attention, Helen calls them, Eliot's having one of his cries for help again. Court summonses for unpaid parking fines appear regularly in the mail. He is given a verbal warning at Cyburbia. His clothes are too big for him. He is finally booked for driving without a seatbelt. He comes home humiliated and pathetic. Fuck off, he says, when Helen asks him how much the fine is and how does he think he's going to pay it. Fuck off and leave me alone. Uh-oh, she thinks. Disintegrating fast.

Every so often she thinks of her screenplay. Sometimes even takes out a pen and paper and sits with them at her desk. There they sit – Helen, the pen, the blank paper, expectant. Waiting for something to happen. Sometimes she gets as far as Mid-shot. Int. Day. After a while she puts the paper back in the drawer.

She wakes one Saturday morning to the sound of hammering. Eliot is out the back nailing two pieces of wood together. It looks like a cross.

—Christ, Eliot. She laughs. —Hey what's this? She mimes chewing the palms of her hands. —Jesus biting his nails.

He looks at her with real dislike. Whoops. Not funny.

—I'm leaving, Helen. I can't stand this.

Wait. Wait a minute. This is not in the script. He does not do this. Not part of the game-plan. Helen starts sweating. She's got to pull this back, fast.

—Eliot.

—Don't want to talk about it. Going. Can't do it.

The sight of him trying not to cry is too much. She sits on the steps below him and clutches his knees. He tries to jerk away.

—Don't leave me, Eliot. I mean it.

—Why not? You hate me. You don't tell me anything. I don't even know you.

—I'm trying to change.

—Not hard enough.

—I will. I promise. I don't want this to end.

I don't want it to end like this, is what she means. With him calling the shots. It's so strange to suddenly look at him as if he's a real person and not just a punching-bag. She wonders how long it will last.

—Promise me you'll change.

—I do promise. I do. Stay?

—Oh, I love you, Hel, he says, sobbing into her hair.

She looks up at the sky, watches an aeroplane passing over. Not long.

Life after Eliot. Because, of course, she leaves him. Has to. That little outburst of his was a catalyst. She can't take the risk of being the one who is left. She thinks back to the party where they met. She knows that Eliot has been in love with

Fantasy Helen, but even that is wearing thin. Helen is certainly bored to tears by her.

Conclusion – even Fantasy Helen isn't lovable. Even when Helen pulls out all the stops and impersonates a selection of heroines from her favourite movies, she isn't worth spending too much time with.

Solution – as far as Eliot goes, she just needs to remove herself. Simple. This in itself will be like a final gift from Mystery Woman – her inexplicable disappearance. But a solution for herself?

When she imagined how it would be, she saw herself waiting at home when he got in from work. On the couch. With a gin. She'd tell him to pour himself one.

—What's the matter, he'd say.

—I've got to tell you something. I'm not who you think I am. And he'd look – what? – as if all his waiting was worthwhile. As if he was at last going to know. As if he couldn't believe she was finally going to reveal herself, couldn't believe he deserved it.

—Don't look like that, she'd say. —It's not what you think.

—But . . .

And they would sit there in silence, they'd sit there and sit there, and after a while she would get up and leave. Unless somehow – somehow – if she could think of something to say that would justify herself, that would make all of the past months have some point for them both, that wouldn't be the horrible anticlimax that the truth really is. The truth. Which is the option that part of her – the only part of her that seems remotely real any more – longs to take. Except the truth would be vetoed by any test-screening audience. 'I thought it was really dumb how there was actually no big secret.' 'I didn't get what it was she was trying to tell the guy.' 'Her life was so normal, what was she so screwed-up about?' 'She should have killed him with the pick-axe.'

It's not an option.

But, if she could bring herself to tell it – what would Eliot say? Would he say, I love you, I love *you*, don't you understand? Or would he be confused, angry, unable to comprehend the gnawing need she'd discovered to re-invent herself? 'It was horrible how she strung that nice guy along all that time for no good reason.' Quite possibly.

Which is why, when the scene played out for real the next night, she stopped after her first line. She drained her gin.

—I know, he said. —I've always known there's something. What is it?

She looked at his face. She put her gin glass down on the table. She swung her feet off the couch and on to the floor. Every movement felt as if it was being made by a machine. Eliot looked like he wanted to say something but knew that he should stay quiet. They waited. The telephone rang. They let it. She couldn't have asked for a better background noise. The ringing of the telephone in the silent room gave her the courage to believe this was all a play, just an act, as everything between them had been an act. It was the sound effect she needed to become who he thought she was, who she wanted to be. It was the cue for her curtain call. She stood and picked up her suitcase from beside the couch.

—Helen . . .

She almost couldn't go through with it. She had a flash of what it would be like once she lost her audience. But his face. His face – eager, expectant, soppy – confirmed absolutely that this was the only thing to do. And when she walked past him and into the hallway and out the door he did not move after her.

And now she wakes to an empty house, in an empty bed, and spends the afternoons in the library, which seems empty, or at the movies, which are empty. She watches only American movies. Nothing subtle, nothing with sub-titles. She's seen *Everything 2*. She plays music constantly. As long as she keeps her head filled with sound and pictures, she's all right. It's only when she walks home at dusk that it all starts to leak out. The empty nights are endless.

## ABOUT THE AUTHOR

Emily Perkins was born in Christchurch, New Zealand, in 1970 and grew up in Auckland and Wellington. She appeared in the soap opera *Open House* for a year before attending the New Zealand Drama School/Te Kura Toi Whakaari o Aotearoa in 1988. She is a graduate of Bill Manhire's writing course at Victoria University, Wellington. She currently lives and works in London. *Not Her Real Name* is her first book.